PHOEBE
NASH

PHOEBE NASH

Girl Warrior

JUSTIN D'ATH

A & C Black • London

Published 2012 by A & C Black
an imprint of Bloomsbury Publishing Plc
50 Bedford Square, London, WC1B 3DP

www.acblack.com
www.bloomsbury.com

First published in Australia in 2010
by Laguna Bay Publishing,
PO Box 260, Mosman, NSW 2088

ISBN 9781-4081-6567-6

A CIP catalogue for this book is available from the British Library.

This book is produced using paper that is made from wood grown
in managed, sustainable forests. It is natural, renewable and
recyclable. The logging and manufacturing processes conform
to the environmental regulations of the country of origin.

Printed and bound by CPI Group (UK) Ltd, Croydon CR0 4YY

1 3 5 7 9 10 8 6 4 2

contents

1 I'm in Africa!   9

2 Tell Sospeter   14

3 Terrorists   19

4 Worryguts   26

5 I will come   31

6 Sospeter   39

7 Safe   44

8 If looks could kill   50

9 Seventh Wonder   59

10 Another country   64

11 More pretty than Hannah Montana   69

12 Mercenaries   75

13 I want to go home!   78

14 In this together   83

15 Growl   89

16 Don't be a crybaby   95

17 Here goes nothing!   101

18 Safe landing   107

19 Girl warrior   110

20 So much to tell us!   114

For Rosie,
who wanted another book
set in Africa.

1

I'm in Africa!

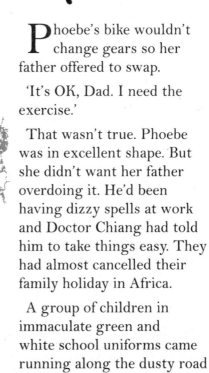

Phoebe's bike wouldn't change gears so her father offered to swap.

'It's OK, Dad. I need the exercise.'

That wasn't true. Phoebe was in excellent shape. But she didn't want her father overdoing it. He'd been having dizzy spells at work and Doctor Chiang had told him to take things easy. They had almost cancelled their family holiday in Africa.

A group of children in immaculate green and white school uniforms came running along the dusty road towards them.

'How are you? How are you?' they called.

'I'm fine,' Phoebe answered. 'How are you?'

'I'm fine,' the children chorused, several of the younger ones giggling and covering their mouths with small brown fingers.

This had been happening all the way from Hippo Camp. Not many tourists visited this part of Zulawi and the local school children all wanted to try out their English on the *wazungus*.

After three days in Africa, Phoebe had picked up several local words. *Wazungu* was Swahili for white people. *Asante* meant thank you. And *jambo* was hello. When they rode past a man leading a donkey with two water-filled jerry cans strapped to its sides, Phoebe gave him a friendly smile.

'*Jambo*,' she said.

'*Jambo*,' he replied, also smiling.

It was amazing to be here. Several times over the past few days, Phoebe had nearly pinched herself to make sure it was real. She wished Sarah and Caitlyn, her two closest school friends, could see her now – riding a beat-up old Mary Poppins bicycle through a real African village!

'Dad, can we take a photo?' Phoebe asked.

Her father leaned his hired bike against a thorn tree and took a photo of Phoebe riding towards him along the dusty dirt road. There was a small, open-fronted shed in the background with several bicycles inside. An assortment of handlebars, wheels, frames and other bicycle parts dangled from the overhang of the roof.

Painted in wobbly white letters above the door was a sign that said, *George's Bicycle Medications.*

'Let's see if George can fix your bike,' Phoebe's father said.

When they explained the problem with the gears, the elderly bicycle mechanic – who was indeed named George – stood the bike upsidedown on its seat and handlebars and spent five minutes tinkering with shifters, pliers and screwdrivers. Then he tipped the bicycle back onto its wheels and took a short test ride up the street, clicking from gear to gear as he went. He came wobbling back towards Phoebe and her father with a big grin on his face.

'It is good now,' George said. 'That will be five hundred shillings, please.'

That sounded like a lot, but Phoebe's father said it was money well spent. 'Now you'll be able to keep up with me on the hills,' he joked.

'Mum said you aren't supposed to ride up hills,' Phoebe reminded him.

Her mother had stayed at the cabin, looking after Connor. Phoebe's little brother had woken that morning with an upset stomach, so he wasn't allowed to go riding. Their mother hadn't wanted her husband to go either – 'Remember what Doctor Chiang said?' she reminded him – but he promised to take it easy. 'Just make sure he does,' Phoebe's mother said to her.

But when you're thirteen, and your father is former world champion cyclist Craig 'Flash' Nash, it's hard to make him ride slowly.

And there was a hill – a big one – just past the village.

'We'll walk up,' Phoebe said, stopping at the bottom.

Her father changed into a lower gear and kept going. 'I'll wait for you at the top,' he said over his shoulder.

'Da-a-ad! You promised Mum you'd take it easy!'

'What she doesn't know won't hurt her,' he called back.

But it might hurt you! Phoebe thought helplessly, as her father cycled away from her up the steep, bumpy hill. She remounted her rattly, old bicycle and set off after him. But only a few metres up the road her front wheel skidded into a rut and she nearly fell off.

That was it. Her father could kill himself if he wanted to, but Phoebe was going to do the sensible thing and walk up the hill.

It was a long climb. Soon her father was no more than a little dot on the skyline, weaving from side to side as he struggled up the last few metres to the hill's crest. Then Phoebe couldn't see him anymore. He must have reached the top.

A tickle of apprehension ran up and down Phoebe's spine. With her father no longer in view, suddenly she found herself alone on the empty road. It was a scary feeling. She was surrounded by bush – African bush. Anything could be watching her from the thorny undergrowth that lined both sides of the narrow road.

Phoebe's fear was irrational and she knew it. Her father would be waiting for her at the top of the hill. Back at the camp they had been warned to stay away from hippos and not to feed the baboons, but nobody had said anything about lions or leopards or hyenas. If there was any *real* danger, wouldn't somebody have said something when they hired the bicycles? Wouldn't they have warned them not to go further than the edge of the village?

I wish I was back in Australia, Phoebe thought.

Then she thought: *Don't be a complete wuss! This is something I can tell Sarah and Caitlyn about when I get home. How I went riding through the African bush on my own!*

Actually, it was kind of peaceful. Now that she was halfway up the hill, there was a good view. Looking back the way she'd come, Phoebe could see the lake where the camp was. On their first day, she and Connor had counted sixty-two hippos from the jetty.

She felt better now. No longer afraid. After all, hippos would never come this far from the water. And there probably weren't any lions or leopards or hyenas so close to a village. When she spotted a pair of cute, little vervet monkeys watching her from the branch of a fever tree, Phoebe waved to them and called out, '*Jambo!*'

She smiled to herself. Talking to monkeys! Just as well Sarah and Caitlyn couldn't see her now.

Phoebe was still smiling as she pushed her bike up the final few metres to the hill's crest.

Then she saw her father, and her smile disappeared.

2

Tell Sospeter

Craig Nash was a big man. When they used to have special events at Phoebe's old primary school – like school plays or sports days – he was always the tallest dad. But lying at the side of the road next to his fallen bicycle, he looked surprisingly small.

Phoebe dropped her own bicycle and ran to him.

'Dad! What happened?' she cried.

His eyelids fluttered a couple of times, then opened all the way. He lifted his head off the road. 'I guess I took a tumble,' he said weakly, giving her a small, lopsided grin. 'These African roads aren't made for bicycles.'

Phoebe helped him to his feet. Red dirt clung to his cheek and jaw where they had made contact with the dusty road, and there was a bubble of spit in the corner of his mouth.

'Are you OK?' she asked.

'Never been better!' said her father, trying to make a joke of it. But when he bent to pick up his bicycle, his legs wobbled and he sat down heavily on the road.

'I guess I'm not OK,' Craig said, looking up at his daughter.

'Is it one of those dizzy spells?'

He nodded. His face – where it wasn't smeared with red African dirt – was deathly pale. 'I don't think I can ride. You'd better go for help.'

Phoebe turned and looked back down the hill. She could see the thatched roofs of the village through the umbrella-shaped acacia trees. It was less than a kilometre away, and all downhill – she could get there in two or three minutes. But she wondered if it was safe to leave her father alone. This was Africa, after all. What if there *were* lions here?

Then she heard a faint rumble in the distance. It sounded like a car. Phoebe shaded her eyes. Yes! A trail of red dust rose above the trees on the far side of the village. It was coming in her direction. Sunlight flashed on a windscreen as a white four-wheel drive broke into view. Whoever it was, they were driving really fast. But they slowed down when they reached the first huts. Phoebe held her breath, hoping they weren't going to stop. But the vehicle kept coming, right through the village and out the other side. Then it speeded up again. It came roaring up the slope towards her.

Phoebe walked to meet it, waving her hands in the air. For a moment she thought it wasn't going to stop. With her heart in her mouth, she stepped right into the middle of the narrow road so it couldn't get past. The driver had no choice. Slamming on the brakes, he brought the dusty Toyota Landcruiser to a standstill less than two metres from where Phoebe stood.

The windscreen was heavily tinted but Phoebe could see two men inside. They were Africans. The driver rolled down his window and beckoned Phoebe forward. He wore dark glasses and had a short, bristly moustache. He looked anything but friendly.

'What do you want?' he snapped.

Phoebe thought it was obvious. Her father was sitting on the road next to his fallen bicycle. 'My father isn't well. Would you be able to take us back to Hippo Camp?'

'We are not going that way,' the unfriendly man said.

'It's only four or five kilometres.'

'We have important business in Biwoti.'

Phoebe had seen a report about Biwoti on last night's BBC news. It had been something about an election, but she hadn't paid much attention.

'Please!' she said, fighting back tears. 'I don't know what to do.'

While Phoebe and the driver were talking, the man in the passenger seat opened his door and got out. He was older than the driver and wore a suit and tie – he looked like someone important. Approaching Phoebe's father, he stooped and spoke softly to him.

'Joseph!' he called over his shoulder.

From the way the driver jumped out of the vehicle and hurried to join him, Phoebe guessed the important-looking man was Joseph's boss. Together, the two Africans lifted Craig Nash to his feet and helped him into the back seat of the Toyota.

'Get in please, young lady,' Joseph's boss said, holding the door open for Phoebe.

She climbed in next to her father. Craig couldn't use his hands properly, so Phoebe helped him buckle up his seatbelt.

'How are you feeling, Dad?'

'Not so good,' he said softly.

There was a loud clatter above their heads as Joseph lifted one of their bicycles onto the Toyota's roof-rack. The important-looking man wheeled the second bicycle over and Joseph swung it up, too. A minute later, Joseph slipped in behind the steering wheel and they were on their way.

But it was the *wrong* way!

'Aren't you going to turn around?' Phoebe asked Joseph. 'Hippo Camp's back there.'

It was his boss who answered. 'We do not have time to go back,' he said apologetically. 'But there is a hospital at Biwoti. It is the best place for your father.'

Phoebe looked at her father. He was resting his head against the seat back, and his eyes were closed.

'Is it far?' she asked.

'Not very far,' Joseph's boss said. He turned to her and smiled. 'You have come to Africa to see the animals?'

She nodded. 'Our safari leaves on Thursday. It was supposed to go two days ago, but there was a delay – some sort of trouble at one of the places where we're going.'

'I must apologise, young lady, on behalf of my country,' the friendly African said gravely. He raised his eyebrows. 'Soon, I hope, things will change.'

'Maybe today,' said Joseph.

The older man laughed. 'It will take more than one day, Joseph. But if God smiles on us next Saturday, it will be a beginning.'

Phoebe was only half-listening to their conversation. There were people on the road ahead. They looked like...

Joseph muttered something in Swahili and put his foot on the brakes. The Toyota skidded to a standstill.

'What do they want?' Phoebe asked.

Three men, dressed like soldiers, stood in the middle of the road, pointing guns straight at them.

'Put this in your pocket, young lady,' Joseph's boss said quietly. Without turning his head, he slipped a small mobile phone back between the seats. 'Tell Sospeter his father loves him.'

Then he opened his door and got out.

3

Terrorists

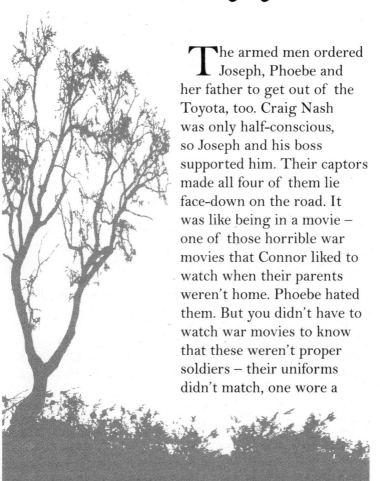

The armed men ordered Joseph, Phoebe and her father to get out of the Toyota, too. Craig Nash was only half-conscious, so Joseph and his boss supported him. Their captors made all four of them lie face-down on the road. It was like being in a movie – one of those horrible war movies that Connor liked to watch when their parents weren't home. Phoebe hated them. But you didn't have to watch war movies to know that these weren't proper soldiers – their uniforms didn't match, one wore a black cowboy hat, and the youngest looked barely older than Phoebe. *They must be terrorists*, she thought. She had never been so scared in her life.

One by one, the terrorists searched them. When they came to her father, he didn't move. The boy terrorist prodded him with his gun.

Phoebe lifted her head. 'Please don't hurt my dad – he's sick.'

The man in the cowboy hat walked over to Phoebe, pointed his gun down at her and shouted in Swahili.

'I only speak English,' she said, fighting back tears.

He shouted at her again, waving the big, ugly weapon in Phoebe's face.

Joseph's boss was lying on the other side of Joseph and Phoebe's father. Phoebe couldn't see him from where she lay, but she heard his voice.

'He is telling you to put your head down, young lady.'

Phoebe lowered her head, but she didn't close her eyes. So she saw what happened next. The terrorist nearest to Joseph's boss lashed out viciously with his boot.

Thud!

There was a grunt of pain.

Tears filled Phoebe's eyes. This time she closed them and pressed her face into the warm African dust, covering her head with her arms. She wished she'd woken up that morning with an upset stomach like Connor, and had to stay in their cabin instead of going for a bicycle ride with her father. She wished she was back at school with Sarah and Caitlyn. She wished she could make herself invisible.

Phoebe's third wish seemed to be working. She was the next in line to be searched, but after the trouble with Joseph's boss – after they *kicked* him for trying to help her – the terrorists seemed to forget all about Phoebe. She heard them talking back and forth in Swahili. She heard one of them give an order, then footsteps moving away from her in the direction of the Toyota. Doors opened and banged closed. A motor started up.

Phoebe didn't dare raise her head until the Toyota had driven away. The terrorists had taken Joseph and his boss, but they'd left Phoebe and her father lying in the middle of the lonely bush road. Phoebe jumped up and crouched over her father.

'Dad, are you OK?'

He opened his eyes, then lifted his head and looked around. 'Where are we?' he said groggily. 'What happened?'

'They stole the Toyota and kidnapped the two men who helped us.'

'Woah there!' said her father. 'Who stole the Toyota?'

'The terrorists,' Phoebe said.

He gave her a strange look. 'Terrorists?'

'I think that's what they were. They had soldiers' uniforms, but they didn't look like proper soldiers. One of them was just a boy.'

'Are you sure you aren't making this up, petal?'

Suddenly Phoebe was angry with him. It wasn't nice being ordered out of a car by men waving guns. It wasn't nice being made to lie on the road, or being yelled at in a language you didn't understand, or having a huge gun waved in your face. It wasn't nice thinking you were about to die.

And it especially wasn't nice, after you'd been through all that, to have your father accuse you of making it up.

'Of course I'm not!' Phoebe snapped. 'Look, here are their boot marks.'

Her father slowly sat up. This time Phoebe didn't help him. 'Wow!' he said. 'What an adventure!'

'It wasn't an adventure,' she growled. 'It was horrible. I thought they were going to shoot us.'

Her father looked contrite. 'Sorry. You're right – it must have been pretty scary. But at least they didn't hurt you.'

They hurt the nice African who tried to help us, Phoebe was about to say, but her father spoke first.

'Help me up, Phoebe.'

'You shouldn't get up,' she said. 'You might pass out again.'

'I can't stay here.'

Phoebe sighed. He was right. And being cross with him wasn't going to help anyone. She hauled her father to his feet, then started brushing the dust and sticks off his filthy clothing. He wobbled.

'Lean against me, Dad,' Phoebe said. 'We'll go over to that tree with the rocks under it.'

They weren't rocks, they were small termite mounds clustered around the base of a tall jackalberry tree, about thirty metres back from the road. Craig sat down with a grunt. He let his breath out in a big sigh and leaned his head back against the tree's rough, grey bark.

'They took our bicycles, too,' Phoebe told him. 'I'll have to walk back to that last village and get help.'

Her father opened his eyelids just wide enough to see her. 'Be careful, pet.'

Phoebe set off back down the road in the direction they'd come. It couldn't have been more than five or six kilometres back to the village where George had fixed her bicycle. She reckoned she could get there in less than an hour.

Or, better still, she might meet another car and flag it down.

No vehicles passed her going in either direction. Phoebe had to walk all the way. But time seemed to pass quickly, because she had lots to think about.

Her father, for example: What was wrong with him? Was he going to be all right? Should she have left him on his own out in the African bush?

And who was the well-dressed African who had stopped to help them? He had looked and acted like someone important.

Something else puzzled her. The important man hadn't seemed surprised when the three armed men stepped out onto the road and stopped the Toyota. It was almost as if he was expecting it.

That reminded her. Feeling in her pocket, Phoebe pulled out the little mobile phone. She turned it over in her hand. It was the same as Caitlyn's, only grey instead of pink. Phoebe tried to remember what the African had said to her as he passed it back between the car seats.

Tell someone his father loves him.

Phoebe couldn't remember the name. It wasn't a name she'd heard before. Kind of like Peter, but different. *Sospeter!* that was it.

Tell Sospeter his father loves him.

Who was Sospeter?

Phoebe opened the phone's address book and started scrolling down. Nearly all the listings were letters: A, CP, E, EB, EL, G, GM, PM. Phoebe guessed they were people's initials. None of the combinations had S in them. Finally, right near the end, there was a name: Winifred.

Phoebe looked at the screen for a few moments, wondering who Winifred was. She pressed CALL.

There were five seconds of silence, then the phone beeped loudly in Phoebe's ear. She looked at the screen. No signal. So much for calling someone to get help. So much for passing on the message about Sospeter. Snapping it closed, Phoebe slipped the phone back into her pocket and kept walking.

It took her nearly an hour and a half to reach the village – much longer than she'd expected. She was hot and tired when she got there, and dying of thirst. If she'd had money, she would have stopped at the little roadside food and drink shop on the outskirts of the village, but she'd left her money belt back in their cabin. A man lounging in the shade next to the soft drinks fridge nodded to her in a friendly way. Phoebe wondered if he would give her a free drink if she told him what had happened, but she was too shy. What if he didn't understand English?

'*Jambo,*' said a woman from the door of a tiny hairdressing shop as Phoebe walked past.

Phoebe stopped in the middle of the street. 'Do you speak English?' she asked.

The woman pointed at Phoebe's long blonde hair and made a snipping motion with her fingers.

'Make beautiful,' she said.

The last thing Phoebe wanted was a haircut. She wished she'd brought her Swahili phrase book so she could make herself understood.

'I need someone to help my dad,' she said, speaking loudly and slowly.

The hairdresser mimed the scissors action again. 'Make beautiful,' she repeated. 'One thousand shilling only.'

'No thanks,' Phoebe said, turning quickly away. She didn't want the woman to see the tears in her eyes. Didn't want her to think it was her fault that Phoebe was upset. It was so frustrating! Her sick father was stuck out in the African bush, depending on her to get help, and she couldn't explain it.

But there was one person who would understand her.

4

Worryguts

George squatted in front of his shop, tightening the spokes on a warped bicycle wheel. He frowned when he recognised her.

'Your bicycle has broken again, miss?'

Phoebe shook her head. 'It's my dad. He needs help.'

George listened without interrupting as Phoebe told her story. Then he stood up and wiped his hands with an oily rag.

'I will get my brother,' he said. 'Akili has a truck.'

Akili looked older than George. And his truck looked

older still. It was like a pickup truck without any sides, and the passenger door wouldn't close properly. At one time it had been painted blue, but now it was mostly the colour of rust. Phoebe sat in the middle, squashed between the two brothers. She clutched a half-empty bottle of spring water in her lap. A full bottle rolled about on the floor under her feet. George had brought them. He had also brought a packet of sweet biscuits, in case she or her father were hungry. Phoebe was hungry, but she was too worried about her father to eat. It was nearly three hours since she'd last seen him. What if he'd fallen unconscious again? What if lions or hyenas had found him? Or even a jackal – they weren't supposed to be dangerous, but if someone was lying unconscious on the ground...

Phoebe was also worried that she wouldn't recognise the spot where she'd left her father – the jackalberry tree he was sheltering under was thirty metres back from the road and surrounded by other, smaller trees. But George's eyes were sharp.

'There!' he said, pointing, and Akili brought the ancient truck to a shuddering halt.

Phoebe's heart hammered with relief. Her father was sitting exactly where she'd left him. He looked OK. He even waved when he saw the truck stop. Rising to his feet, Craig started walking towards them.

But he'd only walked a few paces before he hesitated, took a sideways step, then sank to his knees next to a termite mound.

'Dad!' Phoebe shrieked, leaping out of the truck and sprinting towards him.

George and Akili followed her, bringing one of the water bottles.

'Give him a drink,' the older brother said. 'It is the hot sun of Africa that makes your father fall down.'

Phoebe *wanted* to believe that too much African sun was all that was wrong – but in Australia the sun was just as hot. And then there were her father's dizzy spells, and how he had collapsed three hours earlier when the sun was hardly hot at all. Phoebe crouched over him, shading him with her body as he half-emptied the water bottle in one long, glugging swallow. Then the brothers lifted him to his feet. One on each side, the two Africans helped the tall, stooped white man back to the truck.

They sat him in the front with Phoebe. George hauled himself up onto the back of the truck behind them. Phoebe gave her father another drink as Akili walked round to the driver's side and climbed in.

'Akili, is it far to Biwoti?' she asked.

'Not very far, miss,' he said.

'Can we go there? The man who stopped to give us a lift said they've got a hospital there.'

'I will take you,' Akili said, starting the engine.

Phoebe's father sat forward. 'I don't need to go to a hospital.'

'Dad, you passed out!'

'It's nothing to worry about,' he said. 'I feel fine now.'

'You couldn't even walk to the truck,' Phoebe reminded him.

'I said I'm feeling fine.'

'You should go to a doctor.'

'I don't need a doctor.'

'Just let them check you out,' Phoebe pleaded.

Her father snorted. 'Petal, give me a break. You're as bad as your mother.'

Phoebe took a big breath to control her frustration. OK, so she was like her mother. 'At least Mum looks after herself.'

'I look after myself!' her father said indignantly. 'I'm twice as fit as your mother.'

'Yeah right, Dad! When was the last time Mum had a dizzy spell and passed out?'

'I told you I'm feeling better now.'

'You need to see a doctor.'

'I've already been to a doctor. Doctor Chiang said it was OK to come to Africa.'

'He told you to take it easy,' Phoebe reminded him.

'I am taking it easy,' Craig Nash said, leaning back in the seat with a loud sigh.

All the time she and her father had been arguing, Akili had been sitting patiently at the wheel of the idling truck.

Now he spoke: 'Which way do we go?'

'To Biwoti,' Phoebe said.

Her father shook his head. 'Take us back the other way please, Akili,' he said. 'And if it's not too much trouble, could you drop us at Hippo Tourist Camp, near the Kaivasha turn-off? I'm happy to pay you.'

'No need to pay,' Akili said, turning the truck around.

'*Please*, Dad!' Phoebe tried one final time to reason with him. 'I don't want you to die!'

Craig Nash ruffled his daughter's hair like he used to when she was little. 'Don't be such a worryguts, petal. Nobody's going to die.'

5

I will come

'Of course you need to see a doctor,' Michelle Nash said to her husband as soon as she heard what had happened. 'Look at you – you can hardly stand up.'

It was true. After Akili and George dropped them off at the camp gate, Phoebe had had to help her father down the long, gravel driveway and across the lawn to their cabin.

'It's just a bit of dizzyness,' the former Olympian said, lowering himself onto the cane settee next to his nine-year-old son. Connor was still in his pyjamas, and playing his Nintendo DS as usual. 'Who's winning, champ?' his father asked him.

'Me,' Connor said without looking up. 'I've reached Level Nine, and I've still got all my lives left.'

'Way to go!' said Craig, who looked as though most of *his* lives had been used up.

Michelle caught her daughter's eye. 'Make a sandwich for you and your father, Phoebe. I'm going across to the office to call the police.'

'Why bother the police?' Craig asked tiredly. 'It's over. Phoebe and I are safe.'

'What about the man who was kidnapped?'

He shook his head. 'You're right. I'm not thinking straight. You'd better give them a call.'

'I'll call a taxi, too,' Michelle said as she headed for the door.

'Where are we going?' asked Phoebe.

'I'm taking your father to the hospital.'

Phoebe ate her lunch quickly and got changed. She put on her best jeans, the pretty white top she'd borrowed from Sarah, and the cute white-and-blue ballet flats she bought with her birthday money from Aunty Cathryn. *Who knows, there might be a cute boy at the hospital.* Phoebe imagined swapping email addresses, even getting a photo of the two of them together to show Sarah and Caitlyn when she got home.

Michelle looked hot and bothered when she returned from the office. She hadn't been able to get through to the police, but would try again once they reached the hospital. A taxi was on its way, though.

'Why are you dressed like that?' she asked, noticing Phoebe's change of clothes.

'Because we're going out.'

A look of sympathy crossed Michelle's face. 'I'm sorry, darling. You have to stay here and look after Connor. He isn't well enough to go anywhere.'

Phoebe couldn't believe it. Connor wasn't well enough to go to hospital? That made no sense! 'But—'

'No buts,' her mother said firmly. 'This isn't something we're doing for the fun of it. Your father needs to see a doctor.'

'Maybe Connor needs to see a doctor, too.'

'I hate going to the doctor,' Connor said. 'Anyway, I'm feeling a bit better.'

'So am I,' said Craig, giving his daughter a wink.

There was a knock on the door. The taxi had arrived.

Michelle lifted a hat from a hook on the wall and plonked it on her husband's head. 'You're coming with me, buster.'

'We'll try not to be too long,' she said over her shoulder. 'There's plenty of food and drinks in the fridge, kids. If you need anything else, Phoebe, go and see Mr Ngubi at the office.'

'You never let me babysit back home,' Phoebe said, in a last ditch attempt to change her mother's mind. 'You think I'm too young.'

'Well,' said Michelle, following her husband out the door, 'this is your chance to prove how mature you are.'

Phoebe glared at the closed door for several seconds after her parents had gone. Her father was so wrong to compare her to her mother. Nobody was as mean as Michelle!

Ding-ding-dong, ding-ding-dong, ding-ding-dong!

Phoebe froze. Her eyes swivelled towards the door of the tiny bedroom she was sharing with her brother.

'What's that?' Connor asked.

'What does it sound like?' she said. It was the kidnapped man's phone. She'd left it in there when she got changed. Walking quickly into bedroom, Phoebe picked it up. A name was flashing on the screen: Winifred.

Heart racing, Phoebe pressed the talk button and lifted the phone to her ear.

'Hello?' she said nervously.

Silence.

'Hello,' Phoebe repeated.

Click, the connection was broken.

'Whose phone is that?' Connor asked from the doorway.

Before she could tell him, the phone started ringing again. This time Phoebe tried something different. Raising the tiny phone to her ear, she said:

'*Jambo.*'

There was a short silence, followed by a woman's voice speaking rapidly in Swahili. To Phoebe it meant nothing, except for a name the woman repeated three or four times – Thomas Kipruto. Phoebe guessed it was the well-dressed African's name. The man who'd given her the phone.

'Are you Mrs Kipruto?' Phoebe asked, speaking slowly and clearly, hoping to be understood.

There was another silence. Phoebe thought she heard muffled talking in the background. Then a new voice came on. It sounded like a boy.

'Hello?'

'Hi,' Phoebe answered. 'Do you speak English?'

'Yes,' the boy replied hesitantly. 'Who are you?'

'My name is Phoebe. I'm from Australia. We're here on holiday and—'

'Where is Mr Kipruto?' the boy interrupted. He sounded older now, and slightly aggressive. 'Why are you using Mr Kipruto's phone?'

Phoebe began telling the story. It took a long time because the boy kept stopping her, then speaking in Swahili to someone in the background. Phoebe guessed he was translating what she was saying for the woman who had first answered the phone – Winifred. She must have been the boy's mother. When Phoebe told him about Mr Kipruto's message – *Tell Sospeter his father loves him* – she heard the boy draw in his breath.

'Are you Sospeter?' she asked.

He didn't respond immediately, and when he did, his voice was husky. 'Yes,' he answered. Then he cleared his throat. 'Did my father say anything else?'

Phoebe told Sospeter how Mr Kipruto had translated when the terrorist ordered her to put her head down. But she didn't tell him that his father had been punished – *kicked!* – for speaking to her.

When she'd finished her account, Sospeter asked where she was.

'Hippo Tourist Camp,' Phoebe said. 'It's near the Kaivasha turn-off.'

'I will come,' said the boy, and clicked off.

'What sort of name is Sospeter?' asked Connor, who had overheard Phoebe's half of the conversation.

She shrugged. 'An African name, I guess.'

'How old is he?'

'How should I know?'

'You were talking to him.'

'Well, I didn't ask how old he was.'

Connor drew an imaginary circle on the floor with his big toe. 'Did he sound like he was – you know – about my age?'

'I don't know,' Phoebe said, exasperated. How did a nine year old sound? Annoying, she decided, if Connor was a typical example. 'I guess we'll find out,' she said. 'He's coming here.'

'What for?'

Phoebe hadn't really thought about that. Why *was* Sospeter coming? 'To get his dad's phone, I suppose.'

'I wonder if he's any good at computer games,' Connor said dreamily.

Phoebe rolled her eyes. 'His dad's just been kidnapped by terrorists.'

'So?'

'So I don't think he'll want to play with your stupid Nintendo DS.'

The phone started ringing again. It vibrated in her palm like something alive. Flashing on the screen was a set of initials. *PM*.

'Aren't you going to answer it?' Connor asked after it had rung several times.

Phoebe shook her head. 'It isn't my phone.'

'You answered it before.'

'That time it was Mr Kipruto's wife,' she said. 'This is someone else – someone from his work, probably. They won't want to talk to me.'

'Sospeter's dad *gave* you his phone,' Connor said. 'He must have wanted you to take his calls.'

Phoebe wet her lips, then slowly lifted the phone to her ear.

'Hello,' she said softly.

There was a brief pause, then a deep-voiced man said, 'I am sorry. I must have the wrong number.'

'No, you have the right number,' Phoebe said quickly. 'This is Mr Kipruto's phone.'

Then Phoebe told the man – PM – who she was and what had happened.

When she had finished, PM asked her the same question Sospeter had asked ten minutes earlier:

'Where are you?'

Phoebe told him.

'I will send a helicopter,' PM said.

6

Sospeter

'A *helicopter!*' Connor squawked when she told him. 'That is so cool! Do you think he'll give us a ride?'

'Of course not.' Phoebe was staring at the little mobile phone, hoping nobody else was going to call. 'He just wants to ask me some questions.'

'Why didn't he ask you already?'

'I think he's sending someone else – the police or something.'

'Wow! This is just like a movie!' Connor said.

He was right. But it wasn't the kind of movie Phoebe liked. Or wanted to be in. She was not looking forward to being interviewed by PM's men – especially without her parents there. She opened the little hinged phone.

'Who are you calling?' Connor asked.

'Mum.'

Phoebe punched in her mother's mobile number, remembering to put the international roaming code at the front. But she didn't get through – her parents' taxi must have travelled out of range.

'There's no signal,' she said, slipping the phone into her pocket and moving towards the door. 'Stay here, Connor. I'm just going over to the office to see if I can get the number for the hospital.'

'I'll come with you,' he said.

Phoebe shook her head. 'You're sick, remember? I won't be long.'

She hurried to the office. The manager, Mr Ngubi, was busy at the computer but seemed pleased to see her. He was very helpful. Not only did he look up the hospital's number, but he made the call himself on the office phone. After a long conversation in Swahili, Mr Ngubi put the phone down.

'Your parents have not yet arrived,' he said gravely. 'I have left a message for your mother to phone here.'

Phoebe ran back to their cabin to tell Connor what was going on. Then she returned to the office to await her mother's call.

Mr Ngubi brought a folding chair around from behind the desk and gave her a book about African wildlife to look at. But the text was written in German and after twenty minutes Phoebe had looked at all the pictures three or four times. She stood up and crossed to the desk.

'Excuse me, Mr Ngubi. How far is it to Biwoti?'

He looked up from the computer. 'It is seventy kilometres, madam. One hour in a taxi.'

Phoebe suppressed a sigh. If only he had told her earlier how long she had to wait. *My fault for not asking,* she thought. Back in her seat, Phoebe leaned her head against the wall and closed her eyes. But she wasn't relaxed. At any moment she expected to hear the sound of an approaching helicopter.

Instead, she heard a motorbike.

It pulled up outside the office and the engine fell silent. Half a minute later, the door swung open and a tall, slim African boy came in. He looked too young to have a motorbike licence. Approaching the desk, he addressed Mr Ngubi in a soft voice. He spoke Swahili, but Phoebe heard him mention her name.

She stood up. 'I'm Phoebe Nash,' she said. 'Are you Sospeter?'

When the boy turned to face her, Phoebe was glad she'd put on her best clothes. He was like a younger version of the actor, Will Smith.

'Yes, I am Sospeter,' he said, stepping forward and holding out his hand. 'Hello. I am pleased to meet you.'

Phoebe felt awkward. She had never shaken a boy's hand before. His fingers felt hard, like her father's. Hard and strong.

'I'm pleased to meet you,' Phoebe echoed his words. She felt herself blushing. 'I ... um ... here's your dad's phone.'

'Thank you,' Sospeter said.

'There was a call,' Phoebe told him. 'Someone called PM.'

At the mention of PM, a flash of hope sparked in Sospeter's eyes. 'Has he heard anything?'

'No. Only what I told him. He's sending a helicopter.' Phoebe lowered her voice so Mr Ngubi wouldn't hear. 'I think someone's coming to question me,' she said. 'But I can't tell them anything except what I've already told PM.'

The boy nodded. He lowered his voice, too. 'Can you show me where they kidnapped my father?'

Phoebe chewed her lower lip. She felt sorry for Sospeter – his father had been taken by terrorists – but no way would she ride on the back of a motorbike with a boy who looked barely older than her. 'Shouldn't we wait for the helicopter?' she asked.

'A helicopter makes much wind,' Sospeter said. 'It will put dust over the tracks.'

Phoebe had no idea what he was talking about. But it made no difference – she wasn't going with him. 'Sospeter, I'd really like to help you,' she said, 'but I'm supposed to be looking after my little brother. He's sick, you see. Mum and Dad had to go out and they left me in charge.'

'Where is your brother?'

'Back in our cabin.'

'My mother can look after him,' Sospeter said.

Phoebe was confused. 'How far away do you live?'

'Come,' the boy said. He opened the door for her. 'There is my mother.'

Standing in the shade of a flame tree in the gravel carpark was a small, smartly dressed African woman. A yellow Suzuki motorbike, with two helmets dangling from its handlebars, leaned on its stand next to her.

'My mother wanted to come and meet you,' Sospeter explained. 'She cannot drive a car, so I borrowed the motorbike of my friend.'

Sospeter's mother came forward and spoke earnestly to Phoebe in Swahili.

'My mother asks did the men with guns hurt my father?' Sospeter translated.

'No they didn't,' Phoebe lied. Telling them how one of the terrorists had kicked Mr Kipruto would only make them more worried about him.

'I'll show you where he was kidnapped,' Phoebe said. If Sospeter's mother trusted him enough to let him drive her around on a motorbike, then so would she.

He must be older than he looks, Phoebe thought.

7

Safe

Phoebe tapped Sospeter's shoulder. 'This is the place,' she said, recognising the big jackalberry tree where her father had waited while she went to get help.

Sospeter stopped the Suzuki and held it steady while Phoebe climbed off. Then he got off too and leaned the motorbike onto its side stand. He spent two or three minutes wandering back and forth along the road, his body bent forward, his face intent as he studied the road's dusty surface. Finally he beckoned Phoebe over.

'Four cars have gone past, but here is the mark of my father's shoe.'

As much as she tried to see what he was pointing at, Phoebe could not make out a shoe print in the dust. 'Your eyes are better than mine,' she said.

Sospeter straightened up. 'It is not good eyes, it is how to look,' he said. 'My father taught me. He used to be a tracker.'

Leading her to the side of the road, Sospeter showed Phoebe the blocky tread pattern left by a four-wheel drive tyre.

'Can you see this one?' he asked.

She nodded.

'It is my father's Toyota,' Sospeter said. He returned to the motorbike and pulled on his helmet. 'We will follow it.'

Phoebe hesitated. She had agreed to show Sospeter where the kidnapping happened, but not to join a rescue attempt.

'Do you think it's safe?'

He helped her buckle up her helmet. 'I will take you back to the village. You can wait for me there.'

'No,' Phoebe said. 'I'll come with you. Be careful, that's all.'

They had gone less than half a kilometre when Sospeter braked and did a U-turn. He rode back a short distance, staring down at the road's surface, then stopped and put his feet down to steady the motorbike.

'There,' he said, pointing.

Two sets of tyre tracks left the road and disappeared into the trees. Phoebe recognised the blocky pattern left by Mr Kipruto's Toyota, but the other tracks were unfamiliar – a zigzag pattern, wider and deeper than the ones they'd been following.

'Where are they going?' Phoebe asked. Other than the tyre marks, there was no sign of a trail or a road leading into the trees.

'I will see,' Sospeter said.

He killed the Suzuki's engine and they both climbed off. Sospeter bent to examine the second set of tracks.

'It is a truck,' he said, suddenly whispering. 'Wait here.'

Phoebe shook her head. 'I'm coming with you.'

Sospeter looked at her for a moment, and seemed about to argue. But when Phoebe matched his stare, refusing even to blink, he gave a tiny nod. 'OK. But stay behind me and don't talk.'

It was scary. Phoebe had no idea what to expect. She stayed close behind Sospeter and followed him into the trees. They had only gone a short distance when the boy stopped so abruptly that Phoebe nearly bumped into him. He put a finger to his lips and pointed at a thicket of elephant grass about five metres to their left. Phoebe heard rustling, followed by the snap of a stick. A leafy stem waggled. There was a loud grunt, more rustling, then she saw a flash of brown fur through a gap in the head-high grass. *A lion!* Phoebe thought, and took a step backwards, hitting her head on a prickly branch. A large pig-like animal exploded out of the far end of the thicket and went charging off into the trees with its tail waving in the air like a short, raggedy flag.

'Just a warthog,' Sospeter said.

Phoebe tried to move but her hair was caught on the branch. 'Ouch!' she gasped, trying to free herself from the needle-sharp prickles. But she was well-and-truly stuck.

Sospeter had to untangle her hair. 'This tree is called wait-a-bit thorn. When it catches you, it says "Wait a bit,"' he explained.

Phoebe felt really embarrassed. 'I'm so clumsy.'

'It happens to everybody when they first come to the bush,' Sospeter said, gently freeing the last strand of her hair.

He's nice, Phoebe thought. She wondered if he had a girlfriend.

They found the Toyota fifty metres further into the bush. It was parked under a tree. Branches and clumps of brown grass had been thrown over it so it couldn't be seen from the air. Sospeter made Phoebe hide behind a tree while he crept forward, crouched low to the ground, and peered in through one of the grimy side windows. He straightened up and beckoned to Phoebe.

'Joseph is here,' he called, then pulled open the rear door and climbed in.

Phoebe approached the four-wheel drive nervously. She had a horrible feeling that Mr Kipruto's driver might be hurt, or even dead – that's what would have happened in one of Connor's movies. But to her immense relief, Joseph seemed unharmed. His wrists and ankles were bound with plastic wire-clamps. Sospeter used a pocketknife to cut him free, then he and Phoebe helped the shaken driver out of the Toyota.

'Are you OK?' Phoebe asked.

Joseph wasn't pleased to see her. 'What are you doing here?' he growled, ignoring her question.

'We're looking for Mr Kipruto.'

'It is not your business,' said Mr Kipruto's driver.

'Sospeter asked me to come,' Phoebe said.

Joseph and Sospeter switched to Swahili. Phoebe thought they were talking about her, until the two of them lifted the Toyota's bonnet and looked at the engine. Joseph shook his head in disgust and slammed the bonnet closed. Phoebe guessed that the terrorists had done something to the engine so it would no longer work. Joseph and Sospeter began walking back towards the road, deep in conversation. Phoebe trailed behind them, wondering if they'd forgotten all about her.

When they reached the motorbike there was an argument. Joseph raised his voice and held out his hand to the boy as if he wanted something. Sospeter kept shaking his head and speaking in a normal tone. And he kept his arms folded, refusing to give Joseph whatever it was he was asking for – even when the man started shouting at him. Finally Joseph gave up. Turning away in disgust, he went stomping back along the road in the direction of the village.

'What did he want?' Phoebe asked quietly.

'To take the motorbike,' Sospeter said. He took a deep breath. 'But I said to him it belongs to my friend and Joseph cannot have it.'

'So you told him to walk?'

'True. He is my father's driver, not mine.'

Phoebe was impressed. Joseph wasn't someone she'd want to argue with. 'What do we do now?' she asked.

Sospeter handed Phoebe her helmet. 'We will follow the truck.'

He showed Phoebe how the truck had left two sets of tracks – one leading into the bush, the other leading out.

'Joseph said it was like an army truck, painted green.' Sospeter studied the second set of tracks. 'It has gone towards Biwoti.'

They set off after it on the motorbike. Sospeter rode faster than he had earlier. Phoebe clutched him around the waist. She had only been on a motorbike once before, with Sarah's nineteen-year-old cousin, Bailey. He had taken her around the block, leaning so low on the corners that Phoebe's feet nearly scraped on the road. She had vowed never to go on a motorbike again. But that was before she met Sospeter. He wasn't an idiot like Bailey. Phoebe felt safe riding with him – at least, as safe as it's possible to feel when you're roaring along a bumpy African road in pursuit of a gang of terrorists.

8

If looks could kill

The town of Biwoti was larger than Phoebe had expected, and very busy. The streets bustled with people. There were thousands of them. It was like a street carnival except nobody looked happy. They glared at Phoebe and Sospeter as they zigzagged slowly through the crowd on the Suzuki. Theirs seemed to be the only vehicle using the road.

They rode under a wide banner. It was strung across the street on ropes tied between two buildings. A huge face looked out across the crowded scene below. Phoebe let out an involuntary gasp.

'It's your father!' she cried, tapping Sospeter on the arm.

He turned his head slightly. 'Do not talk so loud,' he warned.

That was when Phoebe noticed the two armed men. They were no more than five metres away, standing beneath the awning of a streetside fruit stall. Both wore green and brown camouflaged uniforms with dark green berets slouched over their right eyes, and both held evil-looking black submachine guns. Instinctively Phoebe knew that these were real soldiers, not terrorists. But they looked just as dangerous. Something in their eyes, as they watched Phoebe ride past on the back of Sospeter's motorbike, sent a shiver down her spine.

If looks could kill, she thought, *I'd be dead.*

There were more soldiers further on. Every ten or fifteen metres another pair stood watching the crowd. Their eyes followed Phoebe with the same creepy look as the first two.

Finally the crowds started to thin. They passed another group of soldiers – six this time – then the street ahead was clear. Sospeter rode for another hundred metres and stopped at a mechanic's shop to buy fuel. There was no petrol pump. Instead, the proprietor – a skinny man wearing a Liverpool Football Club T-shirt and jeans – filled a dented steel watering can from the tap on the side of a 44-gallon drum, then carefully poured the contents into the Suzuki's tank. Sospeter asked the proprietor a question as he got his change, and the man shook his head.

'He has not seen the green truck,' Sospeter told Phoebe.

Phoebe nodded, but she was only half listening. She had noticed a sign with an arrow on it. There was a word written above the arrow. *Hospitali.*

'Does that say hospital?'

'True,' Sospeter said distractedly. 'Wait here.'

Leaving her beside the motorbike, Sospeter walked up the street, questioning other shopkeepers and stall-holders. They all shook their heads. He returned to the motorbike.

'The green truck has not come this way.'

'What will we do?'

'We will go back,' said Sospeter.

'Do we have to?' Phoebe asked, looking back at the crowd and the soldiers.

Sospeter pulled on his helmet. 'We will find a different way,' he said.

They went down the sidestreet where the *hospitali* sign pointed. And sure enough, there it was – a two-storey brick building with a large red cross above the entrance. As they rode past, Phoebe peered up at the blank-looking windows, wondering where her father was. Wondering *how* he was. It felt weird being right outside the hospital where her parents were and them not knowing.

'Mum's going to kill you when she finds out,' Connor had said to Phoebe when she left him in Mrs Kipruto's care back at the cabin.

'She doesn't need to find out,' Phoebe had replied.

But that was before her motorbike ride with Sospeter had turned into a major road trip. When she had thought they would only be gone for half an hour. Now Phoebe didn't know how long they would be away.

Or if she'd *ever* get back.

Phoebe shivered. She could still change her mind. All she had to do was tap Sospeter on the shoulder and ask him to drop her off outside the hospital. She would find her parents and tell them what had happened. Her mother would be pretty angry, but she'd get over it. Words can't kill you.

But bullets can, Phoebe thought. *Terrorists can.*

They reached the end of the street and turned right, into another street, one that would take them around the outskirts of Biwoti and avoid its crowded centre. Phoebe looked at the back of Sospeter's slim brown neck, just in front of her eyes, and thought, *Now's my last chance to get out of this. All I have to do is tap him on the shoulder.*

But she didn't tap him on the shoulder.

After winding their way through a series of backstreets, they arrived back at the point where they had entered the town. The crowds and the soldiers were behind them. Sospeter stopped at three more roadside stalls and spoke to their owners. All three shook their heads.

'The truck did not come to Biwoti,' Sospeter told Phoebe.

'Where is it then?'

He looked back down the road that had brought them to the town. 'There was one turn-off we passed,' he said thoughtfully.

Riding fast, it took them less than ten minutes to get to a place where the road branched in two directions. Phoebe didn't remember passing it earlier, but that was hardly surprising – there was no signpost, and the second road was little more than two wheel-ruts leading off into the scrub at the base of a low hill. Sospeter stopped in the middle of the intersection and peered down at the tracks left by all the vehicles that had passed that way since the last rain. Nearly all of them followed the road to Biwoti. Except the tracks of the truck they'd been following.

And now the tracks of their motorbike.

'Where does this go?' Phoebe shouted at the back of Sospeter's helmet as they roared off down the narrow, unmarked track.

He turned his head slightly. 'Masai Mara.'

Alarm bells rang in Phoebe's head. Masai Mara National Park was where she and her family were supposed to be going. But three days ago there had been some kind of trouble at the border and the area had been closed to tourists.

'It's closed,' she yelled. 'Should we be going there?'

Sospeter slowed down to talk to her. 'I must find my father,' he said over his shoulder.

'Then what will you do?' asked Phoebe. 'There are three gunmen.'

'Joseph said four,' he corrected her. 'One stayed at the truck while the other three kidnapped my father.'

Great, she thought. *Four terrorists.* 'There are only two of us, Sospeter. And they've got guns. I think we should call what's-his-name. PM.'

'The phone will not work here.'

Phoebe rolled her eyes. 'Why didn't we wait for the helicopter?'

'The prime minister can do nothing,' Sospeter said.

What's the prime minister got to do with it? Phoebe was about to ask. Then she got it – PM.

Ohmygosh! She'd spoken to the prime minister!

'Who is your father, Sospeter?'

He turned his head again. 'My father is going to be—'

'Look out!' Phoebe cried.

They had just come around the side of a small, wooded hill and there, in the middle of the track, stood an elephant.

Sospeter slammed on the brakes and the motorbike skidded to a standstill in a big cloud of dust.

The elephant – an enormous bull – had been crossing the road when they came around the corner. Now it turned towards them, tossed its huge head, and charged.

Phoebe screamed.

'Hold on!' Sospeter said.

He shoved the gearbox into first and twisted the throttle. It was lucky he had told Phoebe to hold on, because otherwise she would have fallen off the back. The Suzuki jumped forward so fast that its front wheel rose into the air.

And headed straight towards the charging elephant!

Phoebe clutched Sospeter around the middle and clenched her teeth. What did he think he was doing? When was he going to turn?

But Sospeter didn't turn. Instead, he pressed the horn button and held his collision course with the charging elephant.

He was crazy! Worse than Sarah's cousin! He was going to get them both killed!

At the very last moment, when the elephant loomed over them like a runaway truck, the animal lost its nerve and shied sideways. Sospeter ducked his head and tipped the motorbike the other way. They shot past the elephant, so close that Phoebe could have reached out and touched it – if her arms hadn't been wrapped so tightly around Sospeter.

But suddenly he was the last person in the world Phoebe wanted to hug.

She waited until they were three or four hundred metres past the elephant, then yelled:

'Stop the motorbike!'

Sospeter brought the machine to a standstill. 'Why do we stop?' he asked, looking over his shoulder at her.

'So I can get off,' Phoebe said. But first she checked behind them to make sure the elephant wasn't following.

Sospeter got off too and stood facing her on the dusty road. 'Now you have seen an elephant,' he said.

Phoebe was shaking all over. 'You could have got us killed!'

He shrugged. 'But we are alive.'

'No thanks to you!' she snapped.

Sospeter looked mystified. He seemed to have no idea why she was angry. 'We came too close to that elephant and made him scared,' he said. 'That is why he charged.'

'*It* was scared? How do you think *I* felt?'

'I also was scared,' admitted Sospeter.

'You could have gone the other way,' Phoebe told him.

He shook his head. 'Too close. If I tried to turn, the elephant would have got us,' Sospeter said. He smacked a closed fist into his open left hand to demonstrate the collision between a 7000 kilogram elephant and a puny little motorbike. 'Pow!'

And he actually grinned.

'Sospeter, how old are you?'

'I am fifteen years.'

That explained it. Phoebe unclipped her helmet. 'Here – I'm not about to get myself killed by a fifteen year old.'

Sospeter took the helmet. 'I did not kill you,' he said with a hurt expression. 'I am a good rider.'

'I'm sure you're a very good rider,' Phoebe said. 'But fifteen's too young.'

'How old are you?' he asked.

'Thirteen.'

'Then you should not talk to me like I am a boy.'

'Sorry,' Phoebe said. 'It's just different here, I guess. Where I come from, you *are* still a boy at fifteen.'

Sospeter swung her helmet back and forth in his left hand. He was looking past her, off down the road, and frowning. He must have been thinking about his father.

Phoebe wondered how she'd feel if it was *her* father who had been kidnapped.

'Okay, I'll come with you, Sospeter,' she said softly. 'But please don't play chicken with any more elephants.'

He nodded, but kept staring into the distance. Phoebe turned to look.

At first she mistook it for an early sunset, then she saw it was clouds – a curtain of reddish-brown clouds that stretched all the way across the horizon. But unlike most clouds, these ones seemed to be rising up out of the earth, not coming from the sky. It took a few moments until Phoebe realised it was dust.

'What's causing it?' she asked.

'Wildebeests,' Sospeter said.

9

Seventh Wonder

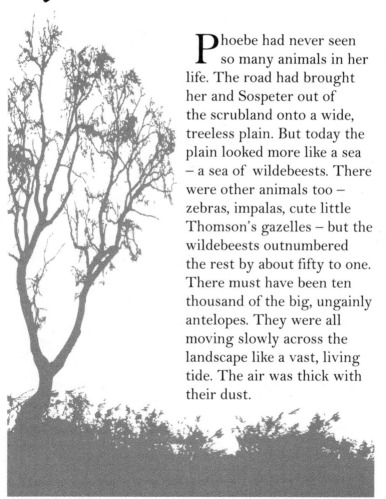

Phoebe had never seen so many animals in her life. The road had brought her and Sospeter out of the scrubland onto a wide, treeless plain. But today the plain looked more like a sea – a sea of wildebeests. There were other animals too – zebras, impalas, cute little Thomson's gazelles – but the wildebeests outnumbered the rest by about fifty to one. There must have been ten thousand of the big, ungainly antelopes. They were all moving slowly across the landscape like a vast, living tide. The air was thick with their dust.

Sospeter slowed the motorbike as they approached the sea of animals. 'It is the Great Migration,' he said, shouting to make himself heard over the thunder of wildebeests' hooves and their strange, sheep-like calls. 'Every year they do this.'

'Cool!' shouted Phoebe. This was one of the sights she and her family had come to Africa to see – their travel agent had called it the Seventh Wonder of the World.

'What does it mean to say "cool"?' Sospeter asked.

'It means amazing, really good, fantastic.'

'Then it is not cool,' Sospeter said. He brought the motorbike to a stop and peered down at the road's hoof-marked surface. 'Now we cannot see where the truck has gone.'

Phoebe understood the problem. The migrating herds had completely obliterated the truck's tyre marks.

'Can't we just follow the road?'

He nodded. 'It is our only chance. But if the truck has turned off this road, we will not know.'

Phoebe watched two baby wildebeests frolicking together like a pair of oversized lambs. 'Maybe we should go back and get in touch with PM,' she suggested. 'It would be easier to find the truck from a helicopter.'

'It is too close to the border – a helicopter cannot go there.'

The alarm bells in Phoebe's head started ringing again. 'What about us?' she asked. 'Isn't there something going on at the border – some kind of trouble?'

Sospeter didn't answer her question. He shoved the gearbox into first and said over his shoulder: 'My father is in trouble, Phoebe. I must find him.'

And then what? she wondered as the motorbike shot forward, scattering wildebeests, gazelles and zebras left and right. What on earth were she and Sospeter going to do when they found the terrorists? *If* they found the terrorists. Part of her hoped they wouldn't. She was too young to die. So was Sospeter. But it was no use arguing with him.

If it was my father, Phoebe thought, *I'd want to rescue him too.*

She thought of her father then, and that made her even more worried. She hoped he was going to be OK.

It wasn't fair. This was meant to be a holiday – Phoebe was supposed to be having fun – but everything was going wrong.

I wish I was back in Australia, Phoebe thought for the second time that day. And this time she absolutely meant it.

But two minutes later she had almost forgotten why she was feeling sorry for herself. So much was going on. There were animals everywhere! Animals you'd normally only see in a zoo. Not only wildebeests, zebras and antelopes, but giraffes, elephants, warthogs, jackals, buffalos and, sitting on a termite mound, two little furry animals that looked like meercats.

And, Phoebe had to admit it, Sospeter was cute.

If Sarah and Caitlyn saw her now – riding on the back of his motorbike across the plains of Africa – they would be so impressed.

Gradually the scenery began to change. There were more trees, bushes and tall, red termite mounds, and it was becoming quite hilly. The dust was clearing. So were the herds of animals. Phoebe looked over Sospeter's shoulder and saw a long, straight stretch of clear road ahead of them. A small family of warthogs watched the motorbike go puttering past. Two graceful impala antelopes chewed at some thorn bushes over to their right. But the main migration – the huge mass of wildebeests, zebras and Thomson's gazelles – was behind them.

Sospeter slowed the Suzuki to a crawl and twisted sideways to look down at the road. Phoebe knew what he was searching for. Tyre marks.

'Can you see anything?' she shouted.

His helmet swung from side to side as he shook his head. 'Too many rocks,' he said, speeding up again.

Phoebe held on tight. The road's surface had changed, too, becoming really bumpy. It rattled her teeth.

'Could you slow down, please!' she called.

Sospeter shook his head and rode faster. Phoebe was beginning to change her mind about him, again. He was as crazy as Sarah's cousin. *He's only fifteen,* she reminded herself. *What did you expect?* They flew over a big rock and landed with such a thump that Phoebe was nearly bounced off the back of the motorbike.

'SOSPETER, SLOW DOWN BEFORE YOU KILL US BOTH!' she yelled.

He didn't slow down. Instead, he tapped her knee and pointed to the left. Phoebe looked that way.

Ohmygosh!

Standing beneath an umbrella tree no more than a hundred metres away was a huge, black-maned lion. Five or six lionesses lay in the shade behind it. Phoebe felt her skin prickle. Those were actual *wild* lions! She wasn't at a zoo watching them from the other side of strong iron bars, or at one of those drive-through wildlife parks, safe inside a safari vehicle. She was in the lions' own territory, on a motorbike.

How fast can lions run? Phoebe wondered.

She hugged the African boy around his slim, muscly waist and held on for her life – literally.

Go Sospeter! she thought.

Although she knew it was silly, Phoebe kept looking over her shoulder long after the lions had disappeared from sight. So when Sospeter tapped her leg again, and pointed ahead of them, it took Phoebe by surprise. She leaned sideways to look over his shoulder, half-expecting to see another lion. All she saw was a low ridge, covered in trees. As much as she strained her eyes, she couldn't see any lions. She hoped Sospeter couldn't either. Then Phoebe shifted her focus upwards. She noticed a faint grey line rising out of the trees at the top of the ridge and drifting off into the late afternoon sky.

'*SMOKE!*' Sospeter yelled.

10

Another country

Phoebe knew what Sospeter was thinking: Where there's smoke, there's fire. And the fire Sospeter was imagining had been lit by his father's kidnappers. They must have stopped and made camp for the night.

The scared part of Phoebe – the part that thought she and Sospeter were too young to die – hoped he was wrong. Phoebe cared about Mr Kipruto – she didn't want him to die, either – but what were their chances of saving him? Especially if

they came roaring into the kidnappers' camp in broad daylight.

She tapped Sospeter on the arm. *'SLOW DOWN!'* she called. *'THEY'LL HEAR US COMING!'*

This time Sospeter listened to her. Not only did he slow the motorbike down, but he stopped altogether and switched off the engine.

'We will walk so they will not hear us,' he said.

They hid the Suzuki and their helmets behind a clump of tall, cactus-like plants and went forward on foot. Phoebe stayed very close to Sospeter. She didn't know which she would rather meet – terrorists or lions?

What am I even doing here? she wondered.

Just before it disappeared into the trees, the road dipped through a dry creekbed. It was sandy in places. Imprinted in the sand were the tyre tracks they'd been following all afternoon. Sospeter turned to Phoebe and gave her a silent thumbs-up. She held up a hand, not really paying attention to him. She could hear voices – men's voices, women's voices and the voices of children. A goat bleated.

Sospeter's shoulders relaxed. 'It is not the ones we are looking for,' he said, leading Phoebe up the slope and into the trees.

The village was on the other side of the ridge. Phoebe and Sospeter walked down a dusty street between two rows of dome-shaped huts. The huts' walls were made of pressed earth, branches and sticks, and their roofs were grass thatch. This village seemed much more primitive than George the bicycle mechanic's, but here and there Phoebe saw signs of the world she had come from. A woman washed her baby in a red plastic bucket. A group of small boys kicked a white football. A car tyre held part of a roof in place.

Here the children didn't wear school uniforms. They didn't smile and call out, 'How are you?' or '*Jambo*'. Instead, they just stared at Phoebe as if they'd never seen a blond-haired girl before. The adults stared too, as curious as their children. It was hard not to feel self-conscious.

Sospeter touched Phoebe's arm, halting her.

'Look,' he pointed.

At the far end of the street – where the village ended – was a tall, barbed wire fence and a double set of gates. Beside the gates stood a sentry box and a flag on a pole. Two men in green and brown uniforms lounged against the wall. Both had submachine guns slung over their shoulders.

'It is the border,' Sospeter said.

Phoebe froze. She remembered how she'd heard there was trouble at the border. The guards were looking in their direction. One dropped his cigarette on the ground and crushed it under his boot.

'I left my passport back at the cabin,' she whispered.

'It does not matter,' said Sospeter. 'Are you hungry?'

Phoebe nodded, unable to take her eyes off the border crossing at the end of the street. It was weird – on the other side of the gates was another country!

'Come,' said Sospeter.

He led her across the street to one of the huts. It looked the same as the others, except for the faded soft drink sign above its door. A man sat on a rickety stool outside. When Sospeter spoke to him, the man disappeared into the hut and came out with two rolled-up pancakes wrapped in brown paper, and a bottle of fizzy lemonade for each of them. Sospeter paid him and handed Phoebe a drink and a pancake. She drank most of the refreshing soft drink so quickly that she barely tasted it, then took a bite of her pancake.

'Did they take your father across the border?' she asked with her mouth full.

Sospeter's mouth was full, too. He shook his head. 'Too dangerous. The soldiers would look in their truck and find him.'

He spoke to the man again. The man nodded and pointed back the way they had come. There was a wide gap between two huts, where another street crossed the one they were on. Sipping his drink, Sospeter walked to the corner and spent a few moments casting about on the ground for tyre tracks.

'The truck was here,' he told Phoebe, showing her a fragment of the now familiar zigzag pattern among all the prints of human feet, dog paws, goat hooves and chicken claws that crisscrossed the village street. 'It did not cross the border. It went this way.'

Phoebe looked where the truck had gone. The intersecting street led out of the village and headed off into the scrub towards the north.

'Where does *that* go?' she asked.

'I do not know,' Sospeter said. 'We will follow them.'

Phoebe glanced at the setting sun. 'It'll be dark soon.'

'So we must hurry,' he said, tugging her wrist. 'Come!'

As they made their way back to the Suzuki, Phoebe tried to talk some sense into Sospeter. 'What are we going to do when it gets dark?' she asked.

'In the dark we can see their campfire.'

'How do you know they'll stop?'

'They must eat and sleep,' Sospeter said simply.

'What about lions?' she asked.

'I am not scared of lions,' he said.

Well, I am, Phoebe thought. 'Could you try the phone again? We should tell someone where we are. My parents will be worried sick – so will your mum.'

Sospeter tried the phone, but there was no signal.

'I think we should go back,' Phoebe persisted. 'It's too dangerous.'

He looked sideways at her. They had reached the Suzuki. 'You are right. It is not your father who is kidnapped. You can stay at the village.'

'No way!'

'They will give you food and a bed.'

Phoebe strapped on her helmet. 'I'm coming with you,' she said.

11

More pretty than Hannah Montana

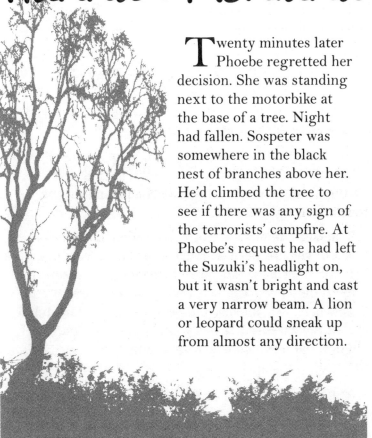

Twenty minutes later Phoebe regretted her decision. She was standing next to the motorbike at the base of a tree. Night had fallen. Sospeter was somewhere in the black nest of branches above her. He'd climbed the tree to see if there was any sign of the terrorists' campfire. At Phoebe's request he had left the Suzuki's headlight on, but it wasn't bright and cast a very narrow beam. A lion or leopard could sneak up from almost any direction.

'Can you see anything, Sospeter?' she asked nervously.

'I need to climb higher.'

'Can you hurry?'

'One more minute,' he said.

There were rustling sounds, and the crackle of branches. Twigs, leaves and bits of bark fell all around Phoebe.

Then Sospeter's voice came again, sounding excited now: 'I can see a fire!'

Phoebe wasn't listening. She couldn't see anything, but she could hear something – more rustling. But this rustling didn't come from the tree above her. It came from out in the darkness.

'Sospeter!' she hissed.

Suddenly Phoebe saw them, right in the beam of the Suzuki's headlight. Eyes! They reflected silver in the light, they were low to the ground, and they were coming straight towards her.

Phoebe could have climbed the tree when Sospeter did, but she had been worried about thorns. Nearly all African trees have thorns. But suddenly the threat of thorns didn't concern her. Phoebe was halfway up the tree when a small black and brown dog came bounding out of the darkness. It was wagging its tail. Above her, high in the tree, Sospeter began laughing.

Phoebe stopped climbing.

Walking into the glow of the Suzuki's headlight was a tall African man wearing a bright red cloak. He stopped beneath the tree and looked up at her. Phoebe recognised his clothing from the brochures their travel agent had given them. He was a Masai tribesman.

'*Jambo,*' he said.

'*Jambo,*' Phoebe replied, feeling foolish as she clutched the tree trunk just a metre above his head. 'Do you speak English?'

The Masai raised one eyebrow. '*Habari?*'

Sospeter translated. 'He says, "How are you?"'

'Embarrassed,' Phoebe said, climbing slowly down. 'I thought his dog was a lion.'

Sospeter climbed down too. He spoke to the Masai in Swahili while Phoebe petted the dog.

'This man saw the truck in the afternoon,' Sospeter told her when he and the Masai had finished speaking. 'They have stopped to make camp not far from here. In the morning he will show us.'

Phoebe was surprised that Sospeter seemed prepared to wait until morning. 'Wouldn't it be better to go now?' she asked. 'If it's dark, we could creep up on them and rescue your father while they're asleep.'

Sospeter shook his head. 'He says there are lions. It is too dangerous. We will stay tonight with his family.'

The Masai village was only a few hundred metres away through the trees. It consisted of six or seven low, igloo-shaped huts inside a *boma*, a two-metre-high fence made from the branches of thorn bushes and prickly trees. The fence looked flimsy, but Sospeter assured Phoebe it would keep the Masais' cattle safe from lions and

leopards. About thirty skinny cows and some long-legged sheep watched them from a smaller pen in the centre of the *boma*.

'What about us?' Phoebe asked.

'You will be in Fatuma's hut,' Sospeter said.

Fatuma was the wife of Wahid, the Masai tribesman who had found them. They had four children – a boy of about Phoebe's age and three pretty daughters with big eyes and even bigger smiles.

'Where will you sleep?' Phoebe asked.

Sospeter puffed his chest out importantly. 'In the men's hut.'

There were four or five other families living within the *boma* and everyone was related in some way or another – brothers, sisters, parents, sisters-in-law, aunties, uncles, grandparents, babies. None of them spoke English, so it was hard for Phoebe to know who belonged in which family, or to remember anyone's name. But the Masai seemed friendly and happy to have unexpected visitors.

Phoebe and Sospeter had arrived at dinnertime, which was lucky because Phoebe was famished. Everyone sat around the cooking fire in a big circle while Fatuma and someone's grandmother served up bowls of steaming vegetable stew and balls of *ugali*, doughy white dumplings that you dipped in the stew and ate with your fingers. It tasted unusual – a bit like soggy tortilla crisps mixed with rice – and was very filling. Phoebe had three helpings.

Wahid watched her eating. He leaned close to Sospeter and said something in Swahili. They both laughed.

'What's he saying?' Phoebe asked.

'He says my yellow-haired wife likes Masai food.'

'Your wife?' Phoebe said, confused.

'He thinks we are married.'

Phoebe felt her face grow hot. 'Tell him we aren't!'

Sospeter said something to Wahid, who studied her across the flames for a few moments, then spoke to Sospeter again. The boy grinned.

'What did he say?' Phoebe asked.

'Nothing.'

'Then why are you smiling?'

Sospeter looked uncomfortable. 'It was a joke.'

'Tell me what it was,' Phoebe insisted.

'He said I should marry you.'

My fault for asking, Phoebe thought. She was glad it was dark and no-one could see her blushing.

'Tell him I'm not even your girlfriend,' she said crossly.

~~~~~

Later, when the meal was over and just Phoebe, Sospeter and Wahid's three daughters remained by the fire, Sospeter apologised on Wahid's behalf for embarrassing her.

'It is different for the Masai people,' he explained. 'Sometimes a girl is married when she is thirteen.'

Phoebe tried not to move. Two of Wahid's daughters knelt behind her, plaiting her hair. The eldest looked about ten. It was weird to think that in just three years' time she might be married. Phoebe wouldn't even be finished school.

'Do you have a girlfriend, Sospeter?'

He poked a stick into the fire. 'There is one girl I like on the television. Hannah Montana.'

'Her real name is Miley Cyrus,' Phoebe said.

'You look like her.'

'She's prettier.'

'No,' said Sospeter, watching the burning stick. 'You are more pretty than Hannah Montana.'

Phoebe felt herself blushing again. She was surprised he had heard of Hannah Montana. Surprised, actually, that he watched television. Then she remembered who Sospeter was – the son of an important man who had his picture on huge banners, who was friends with the prime minister.

'Tell me what's going on, Sospeter,' Phoebe said. 'Who is your father? Why's he been kidnapped by terrorists?'

12

Mercenaries

'They aren't terrorists, they are mercenaries,' Sospeter said.

Phoebe tipped her head back so Wahid's eldest daughter could start another plait from the top. The three girls had no hair at all – their heads were closely shaven like all the Masai women and children – and they loved Phoebe's long blond hair. Even the youngest sister, who looked about three, couldn't stop touching it.

'What's a mercenary?' Phoebe asked.

'They are like terrorists,' explained Sospeter, 'but

someone pays them for what they do. These ones, I think, work for Gerald Kemboti.'

'But isn't he the president?'

'For one more week he is president,' Sospeter said. 'Then there is an election and maybe my father will be president.'

Phoebe gasped. Had she heard him correctly? 'Your father's going to be *president?*'

'If enough people vote for him,' Sospeter said.

Ohmygosh! Phoebe sat forward so quickly that her hair pulled out of the Masai girls' hands. 'Sorry,' she said over her shoulder.

To Sospeter, she said: 'You're serious, aren't you? That's why your father's picture was hanging over the streets of Biwoti – because of next week's elections.'

Sospeter nodded. 'He was supposed to make a speech today in Biwoti. Many people have travelled a long way to hear him. They are angry now at my father because he did not come.'

'It wasn't his fault,' Phoebe said. 'The mercenaries kidnapped him.'

'Yes. Gerald Kemboti paid them to do it. If my father is gone, nobody will vote for him. They will vote for Gerald Kemboti instead.'

'But how can he get away with it? People won't vote for him if he's had your father kidnapped.'

'Nobody can prove he has done it,' Sospeter said. 'That is why the mercenaries released my father's driver. They told Joseph they are being paid by the prime minister.'

Phoebe tried to understand. It was hard to concentrate while three small sets of hands fiddled with her hair. 'Isn't the prime minister friends with your father?'

'True. You see, in this country we have a president *and* a prime minister. It is the president who runs the country, but the prime minister is powerful too. Our prime minister secretly supports my father, and the president wants to get rid of him. If the people believe the prime minister has arranged for my father to be kidnapped, they will not make trouble if the president sacks him. So Gerald Kemboti will not only win the election, he will choose a new prime minister who will support him.'

Phoebe turned her head slightly so one of the girls could begin another plait. 'Will the mercenaries let your father go after the election?' she asked.

'I do not think so,' Sospeter said bleakly. 'My father has many supporters. They would tell the people how Gerald Kemboti has cheated.'

'So what will happen to him?' asked Phoebe.

Sospeter didn't say anything for several seconds. And when he did speak, it wasn't to answer Phoebe's question.

'In the morning,' he said, 'we will go to where the mercenaries are camped and rescue my father.'

13

I want to go home!

They went to bed early. It was barely nine o'clock when Wahid's son led Sospeter away to the men's hut. The three girls led Phoebe to their hut. Its roof was very low. Phoebe had to bend over so she wouldn't bump her head. Once she pushed through the cow-skin door flap, it was pitch black inside – Phoebe could not see a thing. She felt like a blind person. One of the girls took her by the hand and led her to a low platform that must have been a bed. It seemed to be made of sticks covered with animal skins and blankets. Already someone was lying there – they felt too big to be a child. It must have been Fatuma, or the girls' grandmother, or one of their aunts. Phoebe had seen a lot of people – mostly women – going in and out of the hut while they were sitting around the fire. She had to crawl over whoever-it-was to get onto the bed. It was embarrassing. She wanted to apologise or say 'excuse me,' but she didn't know Swahili. The other girls crawled over too, and squashed up against her. There was someone else in the bed with them, on the other side of Phoebe – it felt like another child, perhaps one of the girls' cousins. She wouldn't lie still and kept prodding Phoebe with her bony elbows. Phoebe tried to move away a bit but there wasn't room. They were squashed in like sardines. *At least I won't be cold,* Phoebe thought as someone pulled the skins and blankets over them.

Tired as she was, Phoebe couldn't sleep. Last time she'd shared a bed was at Caitlyn's beach house last summer. Then it had been with one of her two best friends and they'd both had sleeping bags. This time she was with strangers: she didn't know their names; she couldn't talk to them; she didn't even know how many were in the bed! And instead of sleeping bags they had smelly blankets and animal skins!

To make matters worse, the small bony child wouldn't keep still. What a squirmer! Phoebe rolled over so she was facing the other way.

Prod, prod, prod, went a bony elbow, right in the middle of her back.

'Stop it!' Phoebe hissed, trying to nudge the annoying child away with her own elbow.

She felt fur. A wet nose. Teeth. It was an animal! *There was an animal in bed with her!*

Phoebe screamed and jumped up, bashing her head against the low ceiling. Luckily it was soft, made of dried mud mixed with grass. She clambered away from the creature in the pitch darkness, crawling over people in a tangle of legs, arms and blankets.

'There's something in the bed!' she gasped. 'An animal!'

But no-one understood her. They didn't know what was wrong. Stooping so she wouldn't bump her head again, Phoebe felt her way around the wall until she came to the door. Outside there were stars, a small crescent moon and the glowing embers of the fire. Tears blurred Phoebe's eyes as she stumbled over to the dying fire and crouched next to it, panicked, shivering, wishing she was back home in Australia.

There was movement behind her. A black figure emerged from the hut and padded in her direction. It was Fatuma. She put her arms around Phoebe and spoke softly to her in Swahili. Phoebe had no idea what she was saying, but the woman's voice was soothing and motherly. Phoebe wished it was her own mother. But it was nice to be held. Slowly she grew calm. Sniffling, she wiped the tears from her eyes. Fatuma drew her to her feet and tried to lead her back towards the hut.

Phoebe resisted. 'No,' she said, shaking her head. 'Something's in there.'

One of Fatuma's daughers came out of the hut. Her mother spoke to her and she ran off in the other direction. A minute later she returned with Sospeter. He wore a blanket instead of the Western clothes he'd had on earlier, and his feet were bare.

'What has happened?' he asked. 'This girl said you are frightened.'

Phoebe hoped Sospeter couldn't see that she had been crying. 'There's something in the bed,' she explained. 'An animal.'

Sospeter and Fatuma had a brief conversation. The woman disappeared into the hut, then re-emerged carrying a bundle in her arms. It had four dangling legs. With a gasp, Phoebe recognised what it was – a baby goat.

'Its mother is dead,' Sospeter explained. 'They have it in their home to keep it warm in the night time. The Masai value their animals very much.'

Phoebe felt stupid. She had freaked out over a baby goat.

'Tell Fatuma I'm sorry for waking everyone up,' she said.

And for climbing all over them, she thought, but she didn't say that. It was too embarrassing.

When they went back to bed, Fatuma rearranged everyone's sleeping positions so Phoebe was nowhere near the goat. That made Phoebe feel extra stupid. They thought she was scared of it! She wished she could speak Swahili. Then she could explain to Fatuma and her daughters that where she came from – Australia – people didn't share their houses with farm animals. They didn't have to live in huts surrounded by fences made of thorns to keep the lions out. And their beds were soft.

'Back in Australia we're lucky,' Phoebe might have told them.

But she didn't feel lucky tonight. She felt like the loneliest person on earth. Even though she was squashed into a bed with at least four other people and one baby goat.

I want to go home! That was Phoebe's last conscious thought before she fell into an exhausted sleep.

14

In this together

'Did you hear the lion?' Sospeter asked.

It was almost dawn. The eastern horizon glowed orangey-pink where the sun would shortly rise. To the west, a scatter of stars still hung in the sky. Phoebe and Sospeter sat with Wahid and his wife next to the crackling fire. Fatuma had prepared a breakfast of sticky corn meal porridge and sweet, milky tea.

'What lion?' asked Phoebe, still half-asleep.

'In the night,' Sospeter said. 'It was making a big roar.'

'I must have slept through it,' Phoebe said with a shiver. 'Was it close?'

Sospeter shrugged. 'Who can tell? Maybe close, maybe far off. When he roars in the night time, you can hear a lion from ten kilometres.'

Phoebe looked at the flimsy thorn fence. Even ten kilometres was too close, she thought.

'Is it true that they mostly hunt at night?' she asked hopefully.

'Sometimes at night, sometimes in the day,' Sospeter said. He drank the last of his tea. 'Finish your breakfast, Phoebe. Soon we must go.'

They were leaving early so they could reach the mercenaries before they broke camp. That was as far as Sospeter's plan went. He didn't know what they were going to do when they got there. He didn't know how they were going to rescue his father. Wahid had given him a spear. What use would spears be against submachine guns? Phoebe was nervous and Sospeter could see it.

'You stay here with Wahid's family,' he said.

Phoebe was tempted to take his advice. After all, it was Sospeter's father, not hers, who had been kidnapped. She had her own father to worry about. Last time Phoebe had seen him, he'd been on his way to hospital in Biwoti. He should be her number one priority, not some African politician she had only met once. But Phoebe remembered how Mr Kipruto had tried to help her when the mercenaries stopped them. How he'd been kicked for doing it.

'No, Sospeter,' she said. 'I'm coming with you.'

~~~~~~~~

It was too risky riding the motorbike – the mercenaries would hear them coming – so they went on foot. Wahid led the way, then Sospeter, then Phoebe. Both the Masai tribesman and Sospeter carried spears. Phoebe's hands were empty. Not that she would have known how to use a spear anyway. But it would have made her feel less vulnerable. Less helpless. If a lion was following them, it might see the spear and have second thoughts about attacking her. But Sospeter had shaken his head.

'Only warriors can have spears,' he'd said in the deep voice he used when he tried to impress her.

'Says who?' Phoebe had challenged him.

'It is the African custom.'

'You're not a warrior,' Phoebe had said.

'True. But I am nearly a man. I told Wahid I am old enough.'

'You lied to him?' Phoebe had asked.

Sospeter had looked her squarely in the eye. 'It is for my father,' he'd said quietly.

Phoebe could not argue with that. Mr Kipruto's life was in their hands. They had to rescue him somehow.

~~~~~~~~

But when they arrived at the place where the mercenaries had camped, the truck was no longer there.

'We are too late,' Sospeter said, disappointed.

He and Wahid searched the ground for clues. There were the remains of a campfire, still smoking, and some empty soup tins. Someone had smashed a beer bottle against a rock. Wahid kicked dirt over the smouldering campfire, then pointed into the trees ahead of them. He said something and Sospeter nodded. Phoebe could see the familiar zigzag tyre tracks crossing a patch of bare ground. There was no longer a road to follow. The truck had left the road late on the previous afternoon and travelled about two kilometres into the bush, winding its way through the trees until it became too dark for off-road driving. That's when Wahid, returning to his village last night with his cattle, had seen them.

'Where are they going?' Phoebe asked, as Wahid led them into the trees where the truck had gone.

Sospeter shifted his spear nervously from hand to hand. 'Wahid says the border is this way,' he said.

'But you said they wouldn't cross the border,' Phoebe reminded him.

'I said they would not cross where there are soldiers.'

Five minutes later, Phoebe understood. When Sospeter said they were going to the border, Phoebe had expected another town, with a gate and flags and border guards, but here there was just a tall, barbed wire fence in the middle of nowhere.

With a gap in it. Someone had snipped the wires with bolt-cutters and pulled them to one side. The truck's tyre marks went straight through.

'Ohmygosh!' Phoebe said, her heart pounding. 'Why have they taken your father across the border?'

'Because no-one can follow them,' Sospeter said grimly.

He, Wahid and Phoebe stood looking through the damaged fence.

'What are we going to do?' Phoebe asked quietly.

Sospeter took a deep breath. 'We will go back and get the motorbike.'

It took Phoebe a few seconds to understand what he was suggesting. 'No, Sospeter,' she said, shaking her head. 'We can't cross the border. It's illegal!'

He looked her in the eye. 'What they have done to my father also is illegal,' he said calmly.

~~~~~

Phoebe told herself she wasn't going. No way could she cross the border. She didn't have her passport. She had no entry visa. She'd be breaking the law. Phoebe had heard all sorts of frightening stories about what happened to people who broke the law in foreign countries. They got put in prison, sometimes without a trial. Sometimes they simply disappeared.

It was almost too scary to think about.

But Phoebe had to think about it. Sitting on the back of the motorbike, holding the spear awkwardly in one hand (it was alright for her to hold it while he rode, Sospeter said) and clinging to Sospeter with the other, it was the only thing on her mind. They puttered through the trees towards the gap in the fence – the gap that would allow them to travel, illegally, into another country.

Yesterday Connor had said their mum would kill her when she found out Phoebe had gone off with Sospeter on the motorbike. He'd been exaggerating, of course.

But if their mother found out Phoebe was crossing a border illegally, Connor's prediction might not be too far-fetched. Phoebe could imagine her mother's reaction. She'd go totally ballistic.

Well, if I do get in trouble from Mum, Phoebe thought, *at least it'll mean I got back in one piece.*

It was the first time in her life that Phoebe had actually looked forward to her mother's anger.

Sospeter stopped the motorbike ten metres from the gap. He put his feet down to steady the Suzuki, and looked both ways along the fence. Was he having second thoughts? Part of Phoebe hoped he was. If he chickened out now, who would blame him? Nobody would, not even his father. When Mr Kipruto asked Phoebe to pass on his message – Tell Sospeter his father loves him – he hadn't expected his son to try to rescue him. In fact, he would probably be angry at Sospeter for risking his life.

We're both going to get into trouble, Phoebe thought. *No matter what happens.*

It was as if Sospeter could read Phoebe's mind. Twisting his head around, he gave her a nervous grin – a grin that seemed to say, *We're in this together.*

Then he revved the Suzuki's throttle and they shot through the gap in the border fence.

15

Growl

Their surroundings seemed no different – there was the same thorny scrub, the same umbrella-shaped trees, the same red stony ground. There was nothing to show that Phoebe and Sospeter had entered another country.

A tiny dik-dik antelope – hardly larger than a fox terrier – went scampering off through the trees at the sound of the motorbike. Three baboons watched them from a boulder. A huge, eagle-like bird soared high overhead. Borders meant nothing to the wildlife, Phoebe thought. To them it was just a fence.

But for people it was different.

BLAM!

Phoebe got such a fright she nearly fell off the motorbike. Sospeter jumped too. And the baboons fled shrieking from their boulder.

Sospeter swerved the Suzuki under a low thorn tree and switched off the engine.

'What was it?' Phoebe asked, looking in all directions.

'A gun,' he whispered. 'Get off the motorbike, please.'

Phoebe realised she was still clinging to him, even though they had stopped. Quickly she climbed off, nearly stabbing herself in the foot with the spear's sharp steel point. Sospeter climbed off too, and leaned the Suzuki onto its side stand.

'Was someone shooting at us?' Phoebe asked, her heart thumping like a drum solo on fast forward.

'I do not think so,' said Sospeter. He seemed very calm. He removed his helmet, then took off his white T-shirt, stuffed it inside the helmet and placed the helmet on the ground next to the motorbike's front wheel. 'I will go and look. Give me the spear.'

Phoebe handed it over. 'Why have you taken your shirt off?'

'So they will not see me.'

Phoebe looked down at her borrowed top. It was white, too – or had been, when she put it on yesterday. Now it was stained various shades of African brown.

But it was not nearly as brown as Sospeter's dark African skin.

'You stay here,' he said.

Before she could argue, Sospeter turned and went padding away. The last Phoebe saw of him was his slim, brown, bent-over figure, spear in hand, disappearing into the trees. He looked just like a warrior.

And suddenly Phoebe found herself alone.

She had been alone yesterday when she went to get help for her father. But that was different – she'd been on a road, heading towards a village, in a part of Africa where she was allowed to be.

Phoebe waited ten minutes, standing next to the motorbike. She was too scared to sit down, in case a lion or a leopard – or even a baboon – crept up on her. *As if standing up would make any difference*, she thought. And the tree was too thorny to climb.

Please hurry up and come back, Sospeter! she thought.

But after fifteen more minutes, he still hadn't returned. Where was he? Sospeter had told her to wait for him, but she wasn't going to wait all day. *What if he's in some kind of trouble?* Phoebe worried. She decided to give him five more minutes, then she'd go looking for him.

One minute dragged past, then another. Phoebe looked at her watch. She was becoming really worried now. And scared. Scared for herself, and scared for Sospeter. *What if...?*

She never finished that thought. It was interrupted by a shout in the distance – a man's voice uttering a single

Swahili word – followed by two gunshots, one after the other in quick succession. BLAM! BLAM! Then silence.

Ohmygosh! Phoebe thought. *They've shot him!*

Phoebe held her breath, listening for more sounds, but none came. All she could hear was the drumbeat of her racing pulse in her ears, and her chattering teeth. She was trembling uncontrollably, even though the sun was up and it wasn't cold.

Without realising it, Phoebe had picked up Sospeter's T-shirt. She pressed it to her face.

'Sospeter, please don't be dead,' she whispered into the sweaty fabric.

Phoebe waited by the motorbike for another twenty minutes, but still Sospeter didn't return. She knew it was pointless waiting any longer. The shout she had heard, and the two shots, had something to do with Sospeter. He wasn't coming back.

A shadow passed across her. Phoebe looked up. The huge bird she'd seen earlier had been joined by a dozen others. They were flying slowly, around and around, circling high over the trees about three hundred metres away. That was the direction Sospeter had gone. With a shiver, Phoebe realised what kind of birds they were – vultures. Something had died.

Phoebe left the motorbike under the thorn tree and turned her back on the circling vultures. She would go back to the Masai village – provided she could find her way there. Following the Suzuki's tyre tracks, Phoebe began retracing the route she and Sospeter had taken less than an hour earlier. She wished she had a time machine and could turn time backwards. One hour ago Sospeter was still alive. Now he was dead! Phoebe staggered along like a sleepwalker, tears streaming down her face, Sospeter's T-shirt bunched up against her chest. She was hardly aware of her surroundings. All she could think about was Sospeter and how brave he was. How mature he'd seemed for a fifteen year old. And how she would never see him again.

The sound of men's voices snapped Phoebe out of her daze. They were speaking Swahili and seemed to be somewhere ahead of her. Who could it be? Phoebe's heart lurched with excitement. One of the voices sounded like Wahid's.

But something inside her cautioned Phoebe not to jump to conclusions. Instead of rushing forward as her heart instructed, Phoebe's brain steered her feet to one side – behind a thick stand of wait-a-bit thorns growing beneath a yellow-barked fever tree.

Her instincts to be careful were correct. From the safety of the thicket, Phoebe had a view of the damaged section of fence where she and Sospeter had crossed the border.

A brown and green jeep was parked on the other side of the gap. Two soldiers stood guard with submachine guns while four others repaired the fence.

Phoebe watched them from her hiding place, trying to work out what to do. The jeep was on the other side of the fence, so the soldiers were from Zulawi, the country where she and her family were holidaying. If she showed herself and explained what had happened, they might help her. But the soldiers might not understand English. And Phoebe didn't have her passport. She couldn't prove who she was. They might arrest her and lock her up in a tiny jail cell like they did in Connor's movies. What would happen to her then?

That was when Phoebe heard a low, threatening growl.

16

Don't be a crybaby

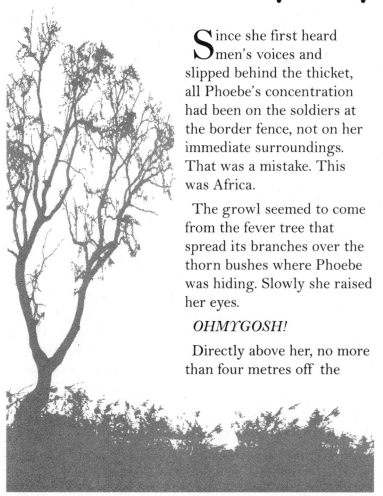

Since she first heard men's voices and slipped behind the thicket, all Phoebe's concentration had been on the soldiers at the border fence, not on her immediate surroundings. That was a mistake. This was Africa.

The growl seemed to come from the fever tree that spread its branches over the thorn bushes where Phoebe was hiding. Slowly she raised her eyes.

OHMYGOSH!

Directly above her, no more than four metres off the

ground – and two and a bit metres from Phoebe – was a real, live leopard!

For three or four seconds, Phoebe didn't move. Nor did the leopard. It was crouched on the carcass of a dead Thomson's gazelle that it must have dragged up into the tree. Then a big drop of blood landed – *splat!* – on Phoebe's arm.

She screamed. And ran out from under the tree. But she had only gone a few paces when something grabbed her shoulder, nearly pulling her off her feet. It felt like claws! Phoebe screamed again and tried to twist away. A long, prickly branch clung to her white cotton top. It wasn't leopard's claws that had stopped her, it was wait-a-bit thorns. But Phoebe wasn't waiting for anything. She pulled harder. Fabric ripped. She ran.

One of the soldiers shouted but Phoebe took no notice. All she could think about was getting away from the leopard. She ran and ran until she was completely out of breath. Even then she kept running. She had no idea which direction she was going, and she didn't care as long as it was away from the leopard. Its cold yellow eyes! Those terrible blood-smeared teeth! Phoebe was sure it was following her. She kept looking over her shoulder, expecting to see it. She kept listening for the pad of its paws on the hard ground behind her. The muscles in her back tensed in anticipation of teeth and claws.

But nothing happened. Finally it was a stitch, not the leopard, that stopped her. It felt like a knife-blade digging into the lower part of her belly. Phoebe stumbled to a standstill and doubled over. Her legs trembled, her shoulders heaved and sweat dribbled into her eyes. Her feet hurt – her silly ballet flats had given her blisters. The top she'd borrowed from Sarah had a huge rip in it. And, worst of all, Sospeter was dead! It was all Phoebe could do to stop herself from crying again.

Don't be a crybaby! said a little voice in her head.

As she slowly regained her breath, Phoebe began to think rationally. Of course the leopard wasn't following her. It already had a meal – *more* than a meal. The Thomson's gazelle was nearly as big as the leopard. All the leopard had been doing, when it growled at Phoebe, was trying to scare her away.

Well, it certainly did scare me! she thought, as she straightened up and took stock of her surroundings.

Where was she? There was thornscrub and trees in all directions. Phoebe looked at the sun – now quite high in the sky. Some people could work out directions from the position of the sun, but Phoebe didn't know how they did it. The sun had been behind them when she and Sospeter set out that morning on the motorbike, so if she faced it she'd be looking back they way they'd come. Or would she? Phoebe wasn't sure. Anyway, she *couldn't* go back because of the soldiers. They had seen her when she ran away from the leopard. One of them had shouted at her. She guessed they hadn't followed because they weren't allowed to cross the border. Phoebe wasn't allowed to, either. She'd be in deep trouble if she went back. Anyway, the fence would probably be fixed by now.

So where could she go?

Nowhere. She was stuck on the wrong side of the border in an African country where she wasn't supposed to be.

And Sospeter was dead.

Phoebe's eyes filled with tears for the second or third time that morning.

'Don't be a crybaby,' she said, out loud this time. Crying wasn't going to change anything. It just made her eyes sore. Phoebe wiped them with Sospeter's T-shirt.

Sorry Sospeter, she thought. And that brought fresh tears. She wiped them away, too. The T-shirt smelt of Sospeter. On impulse, Phoebe dragged it on over her badly torn top. It felt good to be wearing something of his. It made her feel like he was still alive.

Maybe he is still alive, said the voice in Phoebe's head. She had heard a shout and two gunshots, then seen some vultures circling. That didn't prove he was dead.

Phoebe made a decision. She had to find out what had happened. She had to know whether Sospeter was alive or dead.

If he was alive, he might need her help.

Phoebe turned in a slow circle, searching the sky for the vultures. There they were, wheeling high above the treetops about half a kilometre away. Why were they still up in the air? If something was dead, wouldn't they be on the ground, eating it?

Phoebe made her way cautiously towards the circling birds. She walked slowly and stayed alert. Her eyes darted left and right. She tried not to pass too close to any thickets, or to walk under any trees. She didn't want to surprise any more leopards or lions. Or have them surprise her.

There were no surprises – at least, not *animal* surprises.

The big, green truck was parked under a spiky candelabra tree next to some huge, brown boulders.

A man with a gun – he looked like one of the mercenaries from yesterday – sat on the largest boulder. He seemed to be keeping watch. Luckily he was facing in the other direction. Phoebe ducked behind a termite mound. She was no longer worried about leopards and lions. These men were more dangerous than wild animals. Keeping a watchful eye on the man on the boulder, Phoebe edged closer. She darted from one termite mound to the next, she hid behind trees, she crawled through bushes. She used every scrap of cover to conceal her from the mercenaries. Finally she reached a dense thicket fifty metres from the truck and wormed her way into it until she had a good view. Two more mercenaries sat next to a small fire. Phoebe recognised the one with the cowboy hat, and the one who looked like a boy. The fourth mercenary was working on the truck. He had the bonnet propped open with a stick and was doing something to the engine. A scatter of tools, oily rags and engine parts lay on the ground near his feet.

The truck must have broken down, Phoebe realised. That's why the mercenaries had stopped, allowing her and Sospeter to catch up with them at last.

Phoebe shivered and looked at the man sitting on the boulder. The sun glinted on his gun. She didn't want to think about what might have happened to Sospeter.

But now she could see why the vultures were circling – and it wasn't what she had feared. A tripod of sticks had been built over the fire. Skewered on another stick that was tied crosswise inside the tripod, the plucked carcass of a large, plump bird slowly roasted over the flames. From the pile of spotted grey feathers lying on the ground nearby, Phoebe guessed it was a guinea fowl. The mercenaries must have shot it. That explained the first gunshot she and Sospeter had heard – the one that had caused Sospeter to stop the motorbike and go ahead on foot.

But it didn't explain the shout Phoebe had heard twenty-five minutes after he left her, nor the two gunshots that followed. They must have had something to do with Sospeter.

Phoebe studied the truck. Its rear section was fully enclosed in green canvas – like a large rectangular tent. *That's where they must be holding Mr Kipruto prisoner*, she thought. She hoped Sospeter was in there, too. Being a prisoner was better than being dead.

Phoebe stayed in her hiding place for nearly half an hour, trying to decide what to do. The sensible thing would be to go back to the border and tell the soldiers what had happened. There were six soldiers, they outnumbered the mercenaries. If they knew that Mr Kipruto – the man who might be their next president – was being held prisoner in a broken-down truck only a kilometre from the border, they might come and rescue him.

But would any of them speak English? And would they even believe her?

Phoebe knew she couldn't take the risk. If the soldiers didn't understand her, or didn't believe her, she would be arrested. Then there would be no-one to help Mr Kipruto.

Or Sospeter, said the tiny part of her that thought he might still be alive.

17

Here goes nothing!

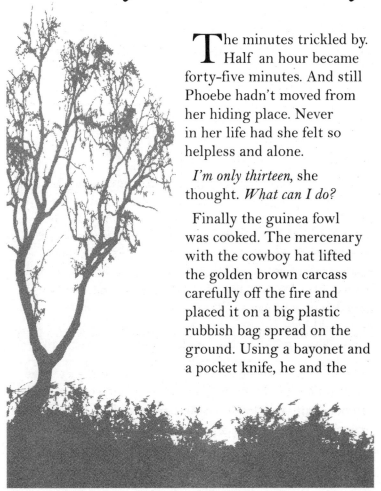

The minutes trickled by. Half an hour became forty-five minutes. And still Phoebe hadn't moved from her hiding place. Never in her life had she felt so helpless and alone.

I'm only thirteen, she thought. *What can I do?*

Finally the guinea fowl was cooked. The mercenary with the cowboy hat lifted the golden brown carcass carefully off the fire and placed it on a big plastic rubbish bag spread on the ground. Using a bayonet and a pocket knife, he and the young mercenary began carving it up. When the cooked bird had been reduced to a big pile of sliced meat and wings and drumsticks, they called to the other two men. The one working on the truck wiped his oily hands on a rag and came over to join them. The lookout slung his gun over his shoulder and climbed down from the boulder. All four sat in a circle and began eating.

Now was Phoebe's chance. Backing carefully out of her hiding place, she circled around to her left until the truck was between her and the seated mercenaries. Then, still using trees and bushes for cover, she crept slowly towards the truck.

I can't believe I'm doing this, Phoebe thought as she picked her way carefully over the dusty, pebble and stick strewn ground. One careless step – the click of two pebbles grinding together under her foot, or the snap of a breaking stick – and the mercenaries would hear her. It would be all over.

But they didn't hear her. Phoebe reached the back of the truck. Up close, it was bigger than she'd thought. Wider and taller. The tailgate was higher than her head. There was a narrow gap at the rear of the canvas like the doorflap of a tent, but Phoebe wasn't tall enough to see in. She could hear the mercenaries talking and laughing only a few metres away. If they looked under the truck, they would see her feet and legs. There was no time to lose.

Here goes nothing! she thought.

Phoebe put one foot on the bumper bar, hooked both hands over the tailgate and hauled herself up and over. Her body parted the canvas flap and she rolled into the truck.

It was dim inside. It took a few seconds for Phoebe's eyes to adjust. The rear of the truck was mostly empty. There were two spare wheels, some jerry cans and a big wooden box. The box looked like the packing crates that valuable artefacts arrived in at the museum where Phoebe's mother worked. It was big enough to fit a person inside. *Or two people*, Phoebe thought hopefully as she crawled towards it. Her heart sank when she saw the padlock. Then she looked closely and realised the padlock was open. Her hands shook and her heart hammered as she carefully undid the latch. She hesitated for a few seconds, dreading what might be inside, then lifted the heavy lid.

A shadowy human form lay in the box's cramped interior. Only one, not two as Phoebe had hoped. Sospeter wasn't there, just his father. Mr Kipruto's hands were tied behind him and there was a cloth gag in his mouth. But his eyes were open. They blinked up at Phoebe in surprise.

Phoebe put a finger to her lips, warning him to keep quiet. *As if he could make any noise with the gag in his mouth*, she realised, and felt a bit silly.

'We've come to rescue you,' she whispered, meaning Sospeter and herself. She didn't know whether Sospeter was alive or dead, but he was the reason she was here.

He had wanted to save his father. Now Phoebe was doing it for him.

When this was over – when she had rescued Mr Kipruto and it was safe to talk – she would tell him something about Sospeter.

Your son loves you, too.

But first she and Mr Kipruto had to get away. She helped him sit up. The mercenaries had gagged him with his own tie. The knot was very tight. Finally, after much struggling, twisting and manoeuvring, Phoebe managed to get it undone. His wrists were bound together with a plastic wire-clamp identical to the one the mercenaries had used on Joseph. Phoebe didn't have a pocketknife to cut the tough plastic.

'Leave me,' whispered Mr Kipruto as Phoebe struggled to undo the wire-clamp with her fingers. 'These are dangerous men. Go for help.'

'I can't,' she replied. 'They brought you across the border.'

Mr Kipruto shook his head. 'I feared this. You should go. This is not your concern.'

Phoebe shook her head, too. 'It is. I'm doing it for Sospeter.'

'How do you know—?' Mr Kipruto began, but he didn't finish the question. Instead, he cocked his head sideways, as though listening to something.

Phoebe couldn't hear anything. Then she realised that was what had distracted Mr Kipruto – there was no longer any noise coming from outside the truck.

The mercenaries had stopped talking.

Suddenly there was a shout – it sounded like a command in Swahili – followed by a burst of gunfire. BLAM! BLAM! BLAM! BLAM! Perhaps Phoebe was mistaken, but both the shout and the gunfire seemed to come from some distance away.

Then she heard footsteps on the other side of the truck. It sounded like someone running.

'Close the lid and hide!' hissed Mr Kipruto.

He lay down in the box and Phoebe quickly closed the lid over him. Then she flattened herself on the floor behind the box where she wouldn't be seen.

The truck rocked. There was the swish of a body pushing in through the canvas flaps, then quick heavy breathing. Phoebe held her own breath. One of the mercenaries had climbed into the back of the truck. He didn't know she was there. But all he had to do was look over the box and he would see her.

There were more noises outside – men's voices in the distance. They seemed to be coming closer. What was going on? Had the mercenaries shot at something and gone to take a look? Why had one of them jumped into the back of the truck? Phoebe wished she knew Swahili so she could understand what the mercenaries were saying.

Suddenly Phoebe's heart skipped a beat. She thought she recognised one of the voices. It sounded like Sospeter! Then, with a sinking feeling in her stomach, she realised her mistake – it was probably just the boy mercenary.

The truck floor creaked. Phoebe heard someone creeping towards her. Uh-oh! For a moment she'd almost forgotten about the fourth mercenary – the one who had climbed into the truck. She closed her eyes and tensed her body, waiting to be discovered. But she was in luck. Instead of looking behind the box, the mercenary opened the lid. It creaked upwards, forming a wooden barrier between Phoebe and the mercenary. He spoke in a whisper to Mr Kipruto – it sounded like a threat – then helped the tied-up man to his feet. Phoebe waited for the mercenary to notice Mr Kipruto's gag had been removed, but he must have had other things on his mind. There was heavy breathing and the rustle of clothing against wood. The box creaked again and shifted slightly as Mr Kipruto got out. Then Phoebe heard two sets of footsteps shuffling away from her.

She peeped around the end of the box.

It was the boy mercenary. With a pistol pointed at Mr Kipruto's back, he marched him towards the rear of the truck. When they reached the flap, the boy pushed the canvas open and forced Mr Kipruto to stand in the opening where those outside could see him. They would also be able to see the pistol, which the boy pressed to the presidential candiate's neck. He shouted to those outside.

The voices fell silent.

Now that the flap was open, Phoebe had a partial view of what was happening out there. Six men with guns stood staring up into the back of the truck. They weren't mercenaries! They wore proper uniforms. Phoebe recognised them. They were the soldiers she'd seen at the fence-border guards from Zulawi.

When the boy mercenary repeated his command, the soldiers dropped their guns.

Then someone else stepped into view.

Phoebe got such a surprise that she forgot about everything else.

'Sospeter!' she gasped.

18
Safe landing

Only after she had uttered Sospeter's name did Phoebe realise what she had done. She had revealed her presence to the boy mercenary. He spun around and pointed the pistol right at her. He yelled in Swahili.

Phoebe bit her lower lip. What was she supposed to do? She was afraid to say anything in case the boy shot her. He looked mad enough – and scared enough – to do anything.

'He says you are to stand up,' Mr Kipruto said calmly.

Phoebe slowly rose to her feet. Once she was upright, she had a better view of what was happening outside the truck. The other three mercenaries lay face-down on the ground with their wrists in handcuffs. The six border guards stood with their hands in the air, their guns lying on the ground at their feet.

But where was Sospeter?

Then Phoebe saw a flicker of movement in some bushes over to the left. Sospeter had ducked out of sight and was creeping towards the truck, using the bushes as cover. He must be hoping to surprise the boy mercenary while he was distracted. Phoebe's eyes darted between the boy with the gun and the boy creeping up on him. She held her breath, hoping the young mercenary wouldn't turn around.

Sudddenly there was a shout. One of the handcuffed men had seen the danger. The boy mercenary turned his head and saw Sospeter coming.

Bumping Mr Kipruto aside, he started to swing the pistol towards Sospeter. Instead of diving for cover, Sospeter leapt out of the bushes and started to run – straight towards the truck!

For Phoebe, everything seemed to happen in slow motion. She knew Sospeter wasn't going to make it. He still had four or five metres to go. No way could he reach the truck before the boy turned all the way around and shot him.

Phoebe was his only hope.

As her body started moving, Phoebe's mind was somewhere else. She saw herself and Sospeter on the motorbike, roaring towards the elephant they had met on the road the previous day. She remembered how terrified she was, and how angry she'd been at Sospeter afterwards. And she remembered what he said: 'I also was scared.'

Phoebe was scared now, as she hurtled towards the boy. She could have done nothing – stayed where she was with her hands in the air. The boy probably wouldn't have harmed her. But she couldn't just stand there and let him shoot Sospeter.

Her mind went blank. It was like the end of a one hundred metres sprint. But instead of a thin strip of white ribbon, waiting at the finishing line of this race was a boy with a pistol. A boy who, at the very last moment, saw her coming and tried to step out of the way.

But he was too late.

Whomp!

Phoebe was a lot smaller than the boy mercenary, but surprise was on her side. And momentum. She hit him so hard he lost his balance and toppled over the tailgate.

Phoebe felt herself falling, too. She knew she should grab the tailgate to stop herself, but somehow the heavy pistol had ended up in her hands and it seemed important not to let go of it. Everything still seemed to move in slow motion as Phoebe tumbled headfirst out of the truck. It was a long, long way down. Far enough, she realised as the ground rushed up to meet her, to break your neck if you didn't land properly.

Luckily Phoebe didn't break her neck.

She landed safely in Sospeter's arms.

19

Girl warrior

While they waited at the border for one of the soldiers to get the motorbike, Captain Gitinji – the one in charge – let Mr Kipruto use his radio telephone to call the prime minister. Then he dialled another number and passed the phone to Phoebe.

'Hello,' said a worried voice on the other end.

'Dad!' gasped Phoebe, who had expected her mother to answer. 'Are you OK?'

'Never been better!' he answered, still her same old

dad. Then he became serious again. 'Phoebe, where are you? We've been worried sick.'

'I'm ...' Phoebe looked around – at the tall barbed wire fence, at a giraffe nibbling the topmost leaves of a thorn tree on the other side of the border, at some vultures circling in the distance. 'I'm not exactly sure,' she admitted. 'But I'm OK. I'm with Mr Kipruto – that man who helped us yesterday – and his son. We're going to get a lift back in the prime minister's helicopter.'

'Talk about having friends in high places!' her father joked. Phoebe heard talking in the background, then her father came back on. 'See you soon, petal,' he said softly. 'Your mother wants to talk to you.'

Uh-oh, Phoebe thought.

'Phoebe?'

'Hi Mum.'

There was a long pause. Phoebe thought she heard sniffling. That was a good sign – if she was teary, her mother mightn't be angry.

She was wrong. Michelle Nash could be happy and angry at the same time.

'Where are you, young lady?'

When her mother called her young lady, it was different to Mr Kipruto doing it.

'I'm not exactly sure. But it's nice here – I can see a giraffe,' Phoebe said. She didn't mention the barbed wire fence or the vultures. 'How's Dad?'

'He's going to be fine,' her mother answered. 'They think it's just a middle-ear infection. But don't change the subject. I want to know, young lady, exactly what—'

That was when the satellite connection failed. Perfect timing.

'Would you like to call back?' Mr Kipruto asked.

Phoebe shook her head. 'I'll see them soon anyway.'

Her mother would get to have her rant. And then she and Phoebe's father would hug her and everything would be all right.

Connor was going to be so jealous about the helicopter ride. *And* the motorbike ride. And seeing all those animals – especially the leopard.

Phoebe hoped her mother would let her keep her hair in the tight little plaits Fatuma's daughers had done for her. And she hoped Sospeter would let her keep his T-shirt. One of the solders had given him an army shirt to wear. He looked good in it – way cuter than Will Smith could ever look.

Before Captain Gitinji drove them to a place far enough from the border for the helicopter to land, Sospeter told Phoebe and his father what had happened after he left her.

He had crept up to within a hundred metres of the mercenaries. But he hadn't seen the one acting as lookout on the boulders. The lookout saw Sospeter, though, and yelled at him to put his hands in the air and come closer. But instead of surrendering, Sospeter ducked back into the trees and ran off. The lookout fired two shots, but both missed. Sospeter hid in some thornscrub while two of the mercenaries searched for him. They found his spear, which he'd dropped when they shot at him, and they presumed he was just a Masai cowherd who had stumbled on them by accident. Then they returned to the truck.

Sospeter spied on them for a while, wondering how to rescue his father. He came up with a plan to create a diversion, but it would take two people – so he went back to get Phoebe. But when he reached the motorbike, she was gone. He followed her footprints, which led him back to the border where the guards were fixing the fence. When he told the guards who he was, and about his father's kidnappers, they agreed to cross the border and help rescue him.

'But the rescue went wrong,' Sospeter said, shaking his head. 'When we caught the mercenaries, one was not there. He was in the truck, hiding. Where you were hiding also, Phoebe.' He smiled at her. 'It would have been a very bad ending if you did not fight him.'

'I didn't fight him,' Phoebe said. 'I just gave him a push.'

Mr Kipruto nodded in approval. 'And it was a very good push, young lady.'

'Like an elephant push,' said his son, slapping one fist into the palm of his other hand. 'Pow!'

Phoebe wasn't sure she liked the comparison. 'Where I come from,' she said, turning her head slightly so they could see her Masai hairstyle, 'girls can be warriors, too.'

20

So much to tell us!

'You *did not* meet the president!' Caitlyn said two weeks later.

Sarah looked disbelieving, too.

'Well, he wasn't the president then,' Phoebe admitted. 'But he got elected the following week. I *did* meet the prime minister, though.'

'Did you get his autograph?' asked Sarah.

'No. But I'm getting a bravery medal.'

'You are *not!*' scoffed Caitlyn. 'Since when did you do anything brave?'

Phoebe shrugged and turned back to her locker. 'If you don't want to hear about it, that's OK,' she said airily.

'That's her!' said a Year Seven boy, walking past with two friends. 'That's the girl who was on *This Morning* yesterday. I told you she went to our school.'

Sarah and Caitlyn looked at the three boys walking away, then turned back to Phoebe.

'You were on TV?' Sarah said.

Phoebe pretended to be busy in her locker. 'I tried to tell you, but you weren't interested.'

'So it's true, then?' said Caitlyn. 'You *did* meet the president of some weird place in Africa, and you *are* getting a medal?'

'A bravery medal,' Phoebe reminded her.

Another boy came past. He was older than the last three, and really cute. He paused near the three girls and pretended to retie one of his shoelaces. When he stood up again, he caught Phoebe's eye.

'You're Phoebe Nash, aren't you?'

'That's right. Who are you?' she asked boldly.

'Sam,' he said. 'I saw you on TV yesterday. That was really brave what you did.'

Then he smiled in a shy kind of way and walked on. Sarah and Caitlyn stood open-mouthed, as if they had just seen Robert Pattinson.

'Do you know who that was?' asked Caitlyn.

Phoebe shrugged. 'He said his name's Sam.'

Her friend nodded. 'He's Sam Fox – the coolest boy in the whole school!'

'And he likes you!' whispered Sarah.

'It must be my new hairstyle,' Phoebe said, touching her plaits.

Caitlyn nudged her arm. 'He doesn't have a girlfriend.'

'That's sad for him,' said Phoebe.

'I could get Loren Featherstone to talk to him for you,' Caitlyn said. 'She's going out with his best friend, Tim Butler.'

'Why would I want anyone to talk to some boy for me?' Phoebe asked.

'To ask if he'd go out with you!'

'But I don't want to go out with Sam what's-his-name. I'm already seeing someone.'

'What?!' shrieked Caitlyn. 'You've got a boyfriend and you haven't told us!'

'Well, he's not exactly a boyfriend,' Phoebe said, embarrassed. 'But we really like each other.'

'Who is he?' asked Caitlyn.

'His name's Sospeter. I met him in Africa. Look, I'm wearing his T-shirt underneath this.'

'He gave you his T-shirt?!' shrieked Sarah.

'That means you two are practically married!' shrieked Caitlyn.

Grabbing Phoebe by one arm each, her two friends began marching her towards their classroom.

'Phoebe Nash, you have *so much to tell us!*' they both said together.

Also available

1

Shot!

A green VW beetle just beat them to the last empty space in the carpark. Mrs Nash had to drive out again and park a hundred metres down the road.

Two police cars swept by as Phoebe got the flowers from the boot. She and her mother had picked them that morning, a selection of waratahs, grevilleas and kangaroo paws from their own garden. Australian flowers for their African visitors.

Phoebe had another gift in the pocket of her hoodie. It was just a little thing she had made herself. She hoped he would like it.

Feeling a bit silly carrying the flowers, Phoebe followed

her mother and little brother along the side of the road towards the airport. Something was going on outside the terminal. A small crowd blocked the roadway where buses and taxis normally pulled in. There were chanting voices and waving signs.

'What are they doing, Mum?' asked Connor.

Michelle Nash shaded her eyes. 'It looks like a demonstration of some kind.'

'Cool!' he said.

Phoebe chewed her lower lip. It wasn't cool, it was very bad timing. Why did there have to be a demonstration on the very day that Sospeter and his mother were arriving?

'Stay close to me, guys,' Michelle said, leading Phoebe and Connor around the edge of the crowd of noisy demonstrators.

Now Phoebe could hear what they were chanting — *'SHAME ZULAWI! SHAME ZULAWI! SHAME ZULAWI!'* — and it gave her a sick feeling in her stomach.

Zulawi was a tiny country in Africa. Hardly anyone in Australia had heard of it until last week, when someone posted a photo on the internet showing the country's new president standing next to a dead rhinoceros, with a gun over his shoulder.

Zulawi's new president was Sospeter's father.

That must be why the demonstrators were at the airport when the president's wife and son were about to arrive, Phoebe realised. To protest about the killing of a rare white rhinoceros.

'*SHAME ZULAWI! SHAME ZULAWI! SHAME ZULAWI!*' they chanted.

It wasn't fair, she thought. Sospeter and his mother had nothing to do with it.

'Stay back, please,' said a policewoman. She was one of about ten police officers keeping the demonstrators back from the terminal doors. 'Nobody's allowed inside.'

'We're not part of the demonstration,' Michelle said. 'We're here to meet someone.'

The policewoman looked at the three of them, then at the flowers Phoebe was holding. 'OK, in you go,' she said, waving them through.

The Nullambine Airport terminal was quite small. Today it seemed too small for the number of people crowded inside. Very few looked like travellers. Instead of luggage and carry-on bags, they carried cameras and microphones and recording equipment. Or they looked like VIPs. Phoebe recognised Ryan McCallister from the Channel 6 News. The mayor was there, too, wearing his mayoral chains. With him were about a dozen important-looking men and women, including Mrs Boothy from the museum, all dressed like guests at a wedding.

'What a circus!' Mrs Boothy said when she saw Phoebe's mother. 'You'd think the Queen was arriving.'

'Well, Mrs Kipruto *is* the president's wife,' Michelle pointed out.

Her boss rolled her eyes. She was wearing a ridiculous crepe hat with a large, fluffy red feather that wobbled when she moved her head. 'That silly man! Why did he have to go and shoot an endangered rhinoceros? Now we'll have to double our security at the opening.'

'I'm sure things will quieten down by the weekend,' Michelle said.

'Let's hope so,' said her boss. 'Otherwise we might have to withdraw the Blue Leopard from the exhibition.'

'No way!' said Connor, standing next to his mother.

Mrs Boothy looked down at him. 'The Blue Leopard is extremely valuable, dear. We can't risk having it stolen or vandalised by the likes of those hoodlums outside.'

'They're not hoodlums,' Phoebe said. Even though she wished they weren't there, she understood the demonstrators' anger. President Kipruto shouldn't have killed a rhinoceros. 'I don't think they'd do anything bad.'

Mrs Boothy smiled at her. It was the kind of smile that a grandparent gives to a little child who has said something cute or silly. 'You must be excited, dear,' she said, 'to be seeing your young man again after all this time.'

Phoebe felt her face turning red. What had her mother been saying about her at work? She hardly knew Sospeter. They had met three months ago when she and her family were holidaying in Zulawi, and they'd spent a couple of days together.

'He isn't my young man,' she muttered softly.

'You email him all the time,' said Connor.

'Mind your own business!'

She wished they hadn't come. Wished their mother hadn't taken her and Connor out of school and brought them to the airport. It was too crowded. Too public. She didn't want to meet Sospeter in front of a thousand people. In front of television cameras! Mrs Boothy was right – it was a bit like a circus.

It became even more like a circus when Sospeter's plane arrived. The other passengers came through first. Then the Arrivals door swished open and the cameras started clicking and flashing as two African men in suits emerged. One was nearly two metres tall and built like a wrestler. The other was small and skinny and wore glasses. Next came Mrs Kipruto wearing a traditional green, red and yellow Zulawi gown, with sandals on her feet and a heavy bead necklace around her neck.

And last came Sospeter in a blue Quicksilver T-shirt.

Phoebe caught her breath. It was the T-shirt she had sent him to replace the one he gave her in Africa. The one that still smelled like him because she wouldn't let her mother wash it.

Sospeter's eyes flicked right and left. He seemed to be looking for her in the crowd. But before Phoebe could catch his eye, the mayor and his welcoming committee – including Mrs Boothy – surged forward. They were followed by all the journalists and photographers. Phoebe, her mother and little brother were left standing at the back.

'Aren't you going to give her the flowers?' Connor asked.

Phoebe shrugged. She wished she hadn't brought them. 'Maybe later,' she said.

They waited two or three minutes. They couldn't see anything, just people's backs and Mrs Boothy's bobbing red feather. Phoebe could hear Ryan McCallister's familiar TV voice asking questions. Mrs Kipruto couldn't speak English, so one of the African men was interpreting. There were several questions about the exhibition, in particular about the Blue Leopard. Then Ryan asked why such a major exhibition was being held in Nullambine.

'It is a very long story,' the interpreter said, translating Mrs Kipruto's reply. 'A girl from this place came to our country and did a very courageous thing. When we have learned that the mother of this girl works at the Nullambine Museum, it is my husband, the president's idea to bring this important exhibition to Nullambine to show the great friendship between your country Australia and our country Zulawi.'

'Who is this girl?' Ryan McCallister asked.

Uh-oh, thought Phoebe.

The fluffy red feather came bobbing through the crowd towards her. The wall of bodies parted and out came Mrs Boothy.

'Come on, dear,' she beckoned. 'It's your moment of glory.'

There was no escape. Mrs Boothy captured Phoebe's hand and towed her into the crush of people. Moments later, she found herself in a small cleared space, facing Mrs Kipruto and Sospeter. They were surrounded by clapping onlookers and flashing cameras. Phoebe's face burned with embarrassment. She had been dreaming of this moment for weeks – rehearsing it with her friends Sarah and Caitlyn – but the reunion she had planned had been nothing like this.

'*Jambo*,' Phoebe whispered, which was hello in their visitors' language.

'*Jambo,*' Mrs Kipruto replied.

'*Jambo,*' said Sospeter.

Phoebe was supposed to do or say something else, but it had gone right out of her head. All she could think about was how stupid she was going to look on tonight's Channel 6 news.

Then she remembered – the flowers!

Stumbling forward, half-blinded by the flashing cameras, Phoebe handed the big bouquet to Sospeter.

Aaaarrrgh! She was supposed to give it to his mother!

Phoebe wished she could simply curl up and disappear.

But she didn't need to. Because suddenly there was a commotion at the other end of the building and everyone forgot about her. A group of demonstrators had found their way in. '*SHAME ZULAWI! SHAME ZULAWI!*' they shouted as they came marching through the terminal, waving their signs and banners above their heads. Police and security staff ran to intercept them. All the cameras, video recorders and microphones swivelled round to catch the action.

Only Phoebe was looking the other way. She was searching for an exit – somewhere to lead Sospeter and his mother in case the police couldn't stop the demonstrators.

Only she saw the man with the gun.

He must have slipped into the terminal while the police and security staff were distracted.

'*LOOK OUT!*' Phoebe yelled.

She threw herself at Sospeter's mother, pushing her out of the way at the very moment the gunman pulled the trigger.

Whap!

It felt like someone had punched her in the ribcage. Phoebe staggered into Sospeter. They both stared in horror at a large red patch that was slowly spreading across the blue fabric of Phoebe's hoodie.

She'd been shot!